THE JUNIOR NOVEL

marvelkids.com

© 2018 MARVEL

Cover design by Ching N. Chan.

Little, Brown and Company
Hachette Book Group
1290 Avenue of the Americas, New York, NY 10104
Visit us at LBYR.com
marvelkids.com

First Edition: January 2018

Little, Brown and Company is a division of Hachette Book Group, Inc. The Little, Brown name and logo are trademarks of Hachette Book Group, Inc.

The publisher is not responsible for websites (or their content) that are not owned by the publisher.

Library of Congress Control Number 2017954745

ISBNs: 978-0-316-41320-6 (paperback), 978-0-316-41797-6 (Scholastic ed.), 978-0-316-41318-3 (ebook)

Printed in the United States of America

LSC-C

10 9 8 7 6 5 4 3 2 1

MARVEL

BLACK PANTHER

THE JUNIOR NOVEL

ADAPTED BY JIM McCANN
WRITTEN BY RYAN COOGLER &
JOE ROBERT COLE
DIRECTED BY RYAN COOGLER
PRODUCED BY KEVIN FEIGE, P.G.A.

LITTLE, BROWN AND COMPANY
New York   Boston

TURN TO PAGE 101 FOR A BONUS STORY FEATURING

MARVEL

BLACK PANTHER

PROLOGUE

The catacombs that lay beneath the Royal Palace in Wakanda were twisty and winding. An easy place for someone to get lost, and for eight-year-old Prince T'Challa and his constant companion, the daring Nakia, the perfect place to race.

"You can't catch me, Nakia!" T'Challa laughed as he darted and wove through the hidden nooks and crannies, as familiar to him as the interior of the palace in which he'd spent his childhood thus far.

Nakia dove into a side alcove, flipped over a pile of crumbled rocks, and emerged back on the main path in front of T'Challa.

"Who says I'm trying to catch you? This is a race, no?" She flashed a sly grin. The chase was on. Running at breakneck speed, both children were unfazed by the outcroppings and pitfalls that surrounded them, instead using them to their advantage to regain the lead over the other.

Light pouring through a large opening ahead indicated that the finish line was in sight. T'Challa and Nakia sprinted toward it. T'Challa ran up the side of the wall and somersaulted over Nakia at the last second, landing just in front of her and reaching the edge of the catacombs and the source of the bright light.

"One day you *will* freeze up, and I *will* race past you," Nakia said hotly.

T'Challa stood proudly. "The prince of Wakanda never freezes."

"Stop where you are," boomed a commanding voice from below. Both children went instantly quiet and stood as still as stones. "Come down from there and enter," the voice ordered.

T'Challa winced. They'd been discovered by the last

person he'd hoped to see. "Yes, Baba," he replied as he and Nakia climbed down from the outcropping to face his father below.

King T'Chaka's feet were planted in the middle of a grand chamber. He was statuesque and regal as always, even when dealing with his mischievous son. "This is the Hall of Kings, my child. A place of honor and respect."

"Yes, Baba," T'Challa replied humbly.

"There are miles of jungle around us for you and Nakia to race through. Use those. When you enter here, you enter holy land. One day, I will join our ancestors here, and you will come pay your respects as I do, seeking guidance in their whispers." T'Chaka placed his hand on his son's shoulder.

"I understand, Baba." T'Challa couldn't imagine a time when his father would not be king, but his young mind comprehended the gravity of the lesson he was being taught.

T'Chaka nodded and smiled, appeased by his son's response. "I have business that calls me from here, but I will leave you alone for a moment to pay your respects to the kings of Wakanda that have come before me, my son."

T'Chaka led Nakia out of the Hall of Kings, leaving T'Challa alone.

PRESENT DAY

A now-grown T'Challa could still hear the footfalls of his and Nakia's impromptu races, still feel the graze of his father's hand on his shoulder, as he looked down upon the newest casket in the Hall of Kings.

"You were right, Father. This hall is one of respect. I only wish I could have brought you home safely from Vienna, as was my responsibility."

T'Challa's hand brushed the casket, his voice catching as a wave of regret washed over him.

From the entry, a guard cleared his throat. "My prince, the Royal Talon Fighter awaits," he said.

Looking back at his father's casket once more, T'Challa closed his eyes and paused in silence. "Thank you for your guidance and that of our ancestors," he said after a moment. "I will strive to be worthy of being not just your son but your successor as well."

Bending to place a brief kiss on the casket, T'Challa turned and followed the guard, leaving his father to his eternal rest in the center of the Hall of Kings.

CHAPTER 1

Chibok, Nigeria

The six trucks in the military convoy wove through the rough terrain of the jungle road like a serpent. In each car, an armed militant sat on the passenger side, weapon pointed outward, scouring the wilderness for any signs of trouble.

Had they looked up and been able to see the camouflaged ship hovering above them, they may have stood a chance.

Inside the Royal Talon Fighter, T'Challa was dressed in his Black Panther gear save for his helmet, which he held in one hand. The pilot, Okoye, was the head of the Dora Milaje, the elite group of warrior women who helped guard Wakanda and were sworn to protect the Royal Family. Okoye was also a lifelong friend of T'Challa's, having witnessed the young boy become the man he was today.

"Have you spoken to her at all since she left?" Okoye asked.

"She said she wanted space," T'Challa replied.

Okoye raised an eyebrow. "For two years?"

T'Challa sighed. "It was foolish, I know."

Okoye walked over to the table composed of black sand-ground vibranium that stood sentry in the center of the RTF. She and T'Challa watched as the sand began to move and reshape itself, forming a model of the convoy below that rose up and out of the table.

"Six vehicles, each with armed guards in the cabs and the trailers," she reported. "The prisoners are in the middle two trucks. She is most likely in one of these two."

"Understood." T'Challa studied the model for a moment longer, paying close attention to the surrounding areas. He then put on his helmet and moved to the center of the RTF. Okoye handed him six round objects, freestanding Kimoyo beads.

"Just don't freeze when you see her," she said, a slight smile crossing her face.

Black Panther took the Kimoyo beads and signaled he was ready. "I never freeze," he said coolly, even as his heart rate increased at the thought that he would see her again, at last.

Okoye nodded, returned to the pilot's chair, and opened a closed fist. With that gesture, the platform beneath Black Panther opened, and he dropped noiselessly from the RTF. Flipping in midair, Black Panther descended through the clouds, graceful as a dancer, with the agility of the sleek leopard that was his mantle's namesake. As he dove, he hurled the beads at the six vehicles. The beads morphed into discs as they made their way to their targets, each one silently attaching to the side of a truck.

Black Panther landed in the brush near the open road and paused. The discs emitted a rippling effect across each of the trucks, and the vehicles simultaneously stopped dead in their tracks.

The drivers of the trucks promptly exited the vehicles,

their faces perplexed and annoyed by the disturbance. Their guards looked around anxiously. A slight whimper of fear came from the back of one of the middle trucks that Okoye had mentioned. A guard walked to the back of that truck and yelled at whoever was inside to be quiet.

Black Panther peered at the middle truck. Nearly a dozen women were clustered in the back; the moonlight reflected off their terrified faces. Accompanying them were two armed guards, one a boy barely older than twelve. He was clearly trying to seem brave.

One of the women in the back of the truck was dressed in the garb of the other Chibok women, but she was not one of them. It was Nakia.

The alert and anxious drivers, coupled with the fact that all six vehicles had stopped at once let her know he was nearby. Which meant it was almost time to act.

Outside, the militants grew increasingly nervous, sensing that some sort of impending threat was making its presence known. From his vantage point in the foliage nearby, Black Panther waited, biding his time until all the militants gathered together.

"There!" shouted one of the drivers, pointing to the brush that was swaying back and forth alongside the road. Two guards cautiously approached the edge of the road, where they could hear rustling. They raised their weapons, readying to fire. Instead, two wild dogs ran onto the road. The guards relaxed and looked back toward the leader of the convoy.

Before they could receive new orders, Black Panther leaped from the trees above, knocking both men out.

"Fire!" the militant leader ordered his men.

Inside the truck, Nakia realized it was time to make her move. She swiftly lunged at the older of the two guards, rendering him unconscious. She turned on the boy guard. He looked frightened, barely tall enough to fit his uniform. Nakia rapidly disarmed him, and the boy fled the vehicle. She looked out the back of the truck and then turned to the other women and signaled that they should get ready to run.

Outside, the militants fired at Black Panther as he tore through their ranks, but the bullets dropped harmlessly to the ground upon impact with his vibranium-laced suit. One by one, the militants fell as Black Panther flipped, dodged, punched, and clawed his way through the group. Using his surroundings to his advantage, he leaped into the trees only to reappear moments later on the other side of the road, constantly keeping his opponents guessing at his next move until it was too late.

Black Panther turned and suddenly found himself face-to-face with the twelve-year-old militant from Nakia's truck. Black Panther raised one arm, claws out, ready to strike, when a familiar voice called out.

"No! Stop! Let him be," Nakia shouted to Black Panther as she began to lead the women from the vehicle.

Suddenly, they heard one of the women scream. A guard was holding her hostage and began yelling at Black Panther. "Demon! I know your stories! The Cat Demon, keeper of souls. You won't have mine!"

Panther crouched, snarling. "Know my stories? Then know my name. I am no Cat Demon. I am Black Panther."

He was about to leap at the man when Okoye suddenly appeared, sliced the man's gun in half with her spear, and then delivered a roundhouse kick that sent him flying.

Looking to Black Panther, she said with a wink, "You froze."

Black Panther rolled his eyes and turned to the boy who stood quivering before them. When he turned to Nakia, his heart caught in his throat at the sight of her. For her part, Nakia tried to hide the look of relief that crossed her face as she gazed upon the man she had not seen in two years. There was an awkward moment of silence, neither sure what to say after so much time and distance apart.

Refocusing on the mission at hand, Black Panther gestured to the boy. "What am I to do with this one?" he asked Nakia.

"These women were all kidnapped from their village. Look at him. They obviously kidnapped him as well and have been forcing him to do their bidding. He's hardly old enough to be held accountable, and I imagine the best thing for him would be a reunion with his family." She looked at the boy and said something to him in his mother tongue. He fervently nodded in agreement and ran over to the women Okoye was helping down from the trucks.

"As you wish, Nakia. Now it is time to return to Wakanda," Black Panther told her.

Nakia was furious. "This is my assignment: freeing these women and others like them. I've been doing this work for two years, and now you swoop in and order me home?"

Removing his mask, T'Challa put his hand on her shoulder, softening his tone. "Nakia, the king, my father … he was killed in an attack in the outside world." Nakia started, visibly shocked by the news. "We tried to reach you before the burial, but you were too deeply embedded in this mission. We couldn't get to you in time."

Nakia drew in a shuddering breath. Her family had always been close with the Royal Family, King T'Chaka like a second father alongside her own. "I'm so sorry, T'Challa. Shuri and Ramonda … how are they?" Nakia asked at length, putting a comforting hand on his arm.

"My sister and mother are strong," Black Panther answered. "The ceremony is at Warrior Falls tomorrow, and the River Tribe Elder requests your presence." He halted a moment before adding, "I wish to have you there as well."

Nakia nodded before breaking away from him and heading back toward the women and Okoye, addressing the huddled group in a Nigerian language. "You are free to go. We will make sure no more men like these come for your village again."

Okoye spoke, also in the women's native language. "There is no need to fear. We have cleared a path back to your village and will watch over you from our plane to guarantee your safe return. Go in peace, my sisters."

As the women and the boy headed into the jungle, Black Panther, Okoye, and Nakia headed to the Royal Talon Fighter. Once inside, T'Challa and Nakia found themselves seated next to each other. The prince opened his mouth to say something, *anything*, but he couldn't find the words to express his feelings at the moment. Fortunately for him, within moments Nakia turned away and curled up, her body language suggesting sleep. T'Challa sighed but said nothing, facing the window to stare unseeing into the inky night. He supposed that whatever they had to say to each other could wait until they touched down in Wakanda.

Facing away from T'Challa, Nakia's wide-open eyes belied her sleeplike position as she searched her heart for the best way to open a long-overdue conversation with her old friend. She, like the prince, was at a loss. As Okoye piloted the RTF into the air, Nakia forced her eyes to close, unaware that T'Challa was watching her, hoping she would speak first.

Amid the silence, the trio took off into the night.

Hundreds of miles later, Nakia had finally fallen asleep—her first decent rest in nearly two years of being undercover. T'Challa's mind was torn between what he knew lay before him in his duties as a member of the Royal Family and the woman who was peacefully resting next to him.

"Sister Nakia, my prince." Okoye's voice cut through the silence. "We are home."

The RTF hovered above a luscious rain forest for a moment before plunging straight down at rapid-fire speed. As they passed the tree line, the forest—a hologram projected across thousands of miles of land—vanished, revealing the nation of Wakanda below. Skyscrapers and buildings were built into the natural jungle landscape, with an intricate, high-tech rail system winding through the streets. The plane headed toward the nation's capital, the bustling Golden City, which harmoniously blended technology with the nature surrounding it.

The RTF made its way to the most opulent building of the Golden City, the Royal Palace. Rising high above all other buildings, the palace encapsulated the meaning of *Golden City*, shimmering even in moonlight as the jewels and gold plating that adorned its exterior caught the lights of the city, making the palace seemingly glow, standing out like a beacon of pride for all the citizens. The RTF landed on the airstrip, which cropped out from an upper level of the majestic dwelling. As the doors opened and T'Challa exited the plane, he was pleased to see his eighteen-year-old younger sister, Shuri, and Ramonda, the Queen Mother, awaiting their arrival, flanked by members of the Dora Milaje.

"Mother, as you can see, there was no cause for alarm. We are all back in one piece," T'Challa said, kissing

Ramonda on both cheeks. "Little sister, you have torn yourself away from your lab to greet me? This is a pleasant surprise," he greeted Shuri, who gave him a hug.

"So? Did he freeze?" she whispered audibly to Okoye as she embraced her brother.

"Like an antelope in headlights," Okoye replied with a slight grin.

"I knew he would," Shuri crowed triumphantly.

T'Challa rolled his eyes at his younger sister. "I didn't freeze," he grumbled, the reply coming out surlier than intended.

Shuri grinned. "Enough about you, brother. I'm here on business—more accurately, for the Kimoyo beads. How did they work? I have some upgrades that could make them better." Shuri was a whirlwind of energy, her complex mind constantly thinking and reworking existing things to create something entirely new. Despite her young age, she was an important and valued member of the highly regarded Wakandan Design Group, responsible for creating some of the nation's most advanced technologies.

"They worked exactly as you made them. Everything was perfectly executed," T'Challa said.

Shuri sighed. "How many times do I have to tell you, brother? Just because something works doesn't mean there isn't room for improvement." She made her way to Okoye.

"Thank you, Princess," Okoye said as she handed the Kimoyo beads to Shuri. "I look forward to what your mind has in store next for these."

Shuri looked at T'Challa and Nakia, who was now paying her condolences to Ramonda.

Ramonda hugged her son after Nakia had walked away. "Thank you for bringing her home safely, T'Challa. It warms my heart to see her."

"She didn't want to leave. If it wasn't for the ceremony tomorrow, I doubt she would have come back," T'Challa told his mother.

Ramonda smiled knowingly. "You brought her. I am certain that had something to do with her decision as well. Nakia is strong-willed, and so are you. Perhaps it is time for you to be more open with your heart?"

T'Challa shrugged, unwilling to let the conversation go in that direction, and promptly shifted the focus. "How are you, Mother?"

"Proud," she answered, her soft smile echoing the sentiment. "Your father and I would talk about this day all the time, and now it has come at last."

T'Challa felt a pang of grief in his heart. "He should be here with us still. This day has come too soon," he said softly.

Ramonda placed her arm around her son. "He is where Bast wills him to be and at the time Bast wills it." She looked at the prince. "Now it is your time to be king, T'Challa."

As they headed into the palace, T'Challa's mind drifted back to his father's casket in the Hall of Kings. Tomorrow, Wakanda would crown a new king. T'Challa hoped he could live up to his father's legacy.

CHAPTER 2

The sun reached its zenith in the azure sky as it gleamed upon the Wakandan River. Barges filled the river, all drifting downstream. Members of all four tribes of Wakanda filled their individual barges: Mining, River, Border, and Merchant Tribes all in full representation. In the rear of the procession, the Royal Barge was lined with both the Kingsguard and the Dora Milaje. On the barge stood Shuri and her friend Ayo, a member of the Dora Milaje.

Shuri was antsy, unused to wearing her regal garments and attending royal events. Give her a white coat over these bells and whistles any day. "I feel like a backup dancer," she told Ayo.

"You are more like Beyoncé here, Princess," Ayo replied with a smile.

Ramonda gave her daughter a reproachful look. "Watch your tongue, girl, and open your eyes." She waved her arm in the direction of the riverbank, where thousands of Wakandans walked, all marching toward the same destination. "Rituals are vital to who we are, and today is about unity. Each tribe will put forth their greatest warrior, who will fight for the throne or willingly choose not to, showing confidence in our family."

"Even you could challenge your brother, Princess," Ayo remarked slyly.

Shuri rolled her eyes. "And be stuck on a throne and deal with elders all day, every day? No thank you. I have my lab; that's kingdom enough for me."

The barges continued to sail downriver before banking near the large waterfall that marked Warrior Falls. The Kingsguard exited the barge and made their way to the foot of the waterfall. As one, they slammed their shields into slots in the ground. The sudden dam diverted the flow of water, and the pool below drained, revealing the Challenge Arena. Rows and rows of seating were carved into the stone pool, all facing a large area where the challengers would compete to become the next king of Wakanda.

The Royal Family took their seats, and the rest of the area began to fill with Wakandans, all eager for the day's events. Each tribe sat in their designated section. Shuri looked over at the River Tribe and saw Nakia seated among her people. She gave a small wave. Above the pool, the thousands of Wakandans who had walked to Warrior Falls lined the area, standing shoulder-to-shoulder, all vying for a view of the proceedings.

A man of about fifty entered the center group. He was Zuri, the High Shaman, carrying with him the Spear of Bashenga. An elder and a chosen warrior from each tribe entered the Challenge Pool. The shaman raised his spear.

"I, Zuri, son of Badu, welcome you all, the tribes of Wakanda, to the Challenge ritual. Representatives of each tribe are present, as is called upon," he said, surveying the members of the four tribes joining him. "I now give to you Prince T'Challa, the Black Panther!"

From above, a Royal Talon Fighter descended, and T'Challa dropped down onto the surface of the arena. He entered the Challenge Pool. He was not wearing his Black Panther garb. Rather, he was covered in leopard body paint and carried a short spear and a shield. He surveyed the enormous crowd gathered to watch his fate unfold.

From her seat among the River Tribe, Nakia studied T'Challa. She doubted few, if anyone, apart from her, could tell that under the confident, determined attitude he was trying to project, he looked slightly overwhelmed. She smiled, knowing how uncomfortable all the attention was probably making him.

T'Challa walked over to Zuri and bowed. Zuri held a ceremonial vessel in his hand and presented it to T'Challa. "Drink this, Prince T'Challa, and the powers granted you by the Panther god will be stripped from your body so that you may equally combat any who challenge you."

T'Challa took the vessel and drank. Within seconds he could feel a burning sensation course through his body. As the liquid took effect, he looked down to see the veins in his arms darkening and bulging. He could feel the herb racing through him, relieving him of his Black Panther powers.

He faced Zuri, handing the vessel back to the shaman.

Zuri reached into a pouch and pulled out a panther mask. He held it out to T'Challa, who took it and placed it over his face.

Zuri addressed the assembled masses. "Victory in ritual combat comes by yield or death. Should anyone try to interfere, they must pay with their life. So now I offer a path to the throne. Does any tribe wish to put forth a warrior?"

"The Mining Tribe declines to challenge the prince," said the tribe elder. Zuri acknowledged the decree with a nod, and the Mining Tribe's warrior and elder took their seats among their people.

One by one, the other three tribes—Border, River, and Merchant—all followed the Mining Tribe in declining to challenge the throne. After the final tribe had taken their seat, Zuri turned back to T'Challa, holding the crown in his hands.

"Tribes of Wakanda, without challenge, Prince T'Challa is—" Zuri's coronation speech was interrupted by the sounds of a steady drumbeat that suddenly filled the arena.

Six warriors appeared and made their way down to the Challenge Pool arena, flanked by two drummers pounding out a beat on their wooden instruments. The warriors were adorned in wooden armor and wielded long wooden spears. In the center of the group, the largest of the warriors had a gorilla mask covering his face.

The crowd reacted in shock at the sight, breaking out into slightly panicked murmurs as the warrior approached Zuri and lifted his mask, revealing a sneer and eyes filled with deep loathing. The shaman looked at the warrior with disdain. "How dare you interfere with today's ceremony," Zuri murmured, shaking his head.

"I, M'Baku, leader of the Jabari clan, demand representation at these proceedings today. No longer will our voices be silenced!" he bellowed for all to hear.

"We made an agreement with your tribe to leave you to your mountains, and you would leave us in peace," Zuri countered.

M'Baku glared at the shaman and began to pace the arena as he spoke. "An agreement made thousands of years ago, witch doctor! Today is a new day. We have watched and listened from the mountains. We heard of T'Challa's trips to engage with outsiders. We watched with disgust as your technological developments have been overseen by a child who scoffs at tradition."

In her seat, Shuri stiffened as M'Baku made intentional eye contact with her. Ayo stepped in front of the Royal Family. M'Baku made his way to stand face-to-face with T'Challa. "And now you want to hand the nation over to this prince, who could not even keep his own father safe?" T'Challa clenched his fist at the sharp insult, but he said nothing. "We will not stand for it!"

M'Baku made his way to the center of the arena. "I, M'Baku, leader of the Jabari clan, wish to challenge for the throne!" The drummers began their pounding again in a fast, rhythmic beat.

Zuri looked to T'Challa, rendered speechless, unsure of how to proceed.

T'Challa stepped forward and stretched one hand toward M'Baku. He looked directly at his challenger. "I accept."

Ignoring T'Challa's outstretched hand, M'Baku placed the gorilla mask over his face again, slammed his spear into the ground, and yelled for all to hear, "Glory to Hanuman!"

Zuri left the Challenge Pool arena to take his place among the Royal Family as the two opponents began to circle each other, waiting to see who would make the first move. The Jabari warriors and the Dora Milaje faced off on opposite sides of the pool, both groups with spears raised.

Without warning, M'Baku lunged at T'Challa. The much-larger warrior landed a nasty blow to the prince's chest, knocking him off his feet. M'Baku leaped toward the fallen Wakandan and raised his spear, but T'Challa swiftly rolled to the side before M'Baku could make contact again. The prince kicked at M'Baku's leg, knocking the Jabari warrior momentarily off balance. With each hit, the Jabari and Dora moved a step closer, forcing the two fighters closer toward the edge of the Pool.

Jumping to his feet, T'Challa swung his leg around and kicked M'Baku's stomach. The challenger grunted in pain but quickly recovered, rage in his eyes. He sprang high into the air, and T'Challa went flying as M'Baku's foot connected with the prince's head. T'Challa dropped both his spear and his shield upon the impact. His ears ringing, T'Challa momentarily lost his balance and fell to the ground. Without his Black Panther abilities, T'Challa was not as physically powerful as M'Baku. He felt vulnerable and wondered how long he could keep the Jabari warrior at bay, much less defeat him. He had barely caught his breath when M'Baku was upon him once more, the two now even closer to the edge than before.

In the stands, Shuri looked worriedly at her mother. Ramonda raised her hand slightly. "He will win. He must simply find the strength we all know is inside him. For his family. For Wakanda."

Shuri stood, raising her voice so her brother could hear her. "C'mon, T'Challa! Kick his butt back to the mountains!"

Nearby, Nakia began to cheer, "T'Challa! T'Challa!" Ramonda, Shuri, Ayo, and Okoye began to echo her encouragement. Soon the chant spread among all the Wakandan people, urging their would-be leader onward.

Still on the ground, T'Challa was being pummeled by M'Baku. Through the buzzing in his head, he began to hear the cheers of his family and friends, of his nation. He ducked away from M'Baku's fist, and the warrior's hand connected hard with the unyielding ground. T'Challa regained enough strength to grab M'Baku's spear. As the two men struggled for control of the weapon, it snapped in half.

T'Challa rolled away and snatched up his own fallen

spear as the Dora and Jabari took yet another step forward. In one fluid motion, he pivoted and struck M'Baku's thigh. The large man roared in pain. The crowd cheered louder as T'Challa leaped into the air and wrapped his legs around M'Baku's neck, toppling the warrior to the ground. T'Challa rolled across the length of the Challenge Pool, around and around, his legs like a vise around M'Baku's neck.

"Yield!" T'Challa yelled to his foe.

"N-never," M'Baku croaked out defiantly.

T'Challa applied more pressure. "I will not kill you, M'Baku! You *must* yield! Not for me, but for the people whose very existence depends on you! They need you. Please, for them—yield."

But M'Baku just continued to struggle. They were nearly entirely outside the Pool now. T'Challa's leg muscles rippled as they tightened and refused to give way.

"M'Baku," T'Challa implored one last time. "Please. For your tribesmen."

Finally, after a long pause, M'Baku raised his hand and tapped the ground twice, indicating his surrender. T'Challa tentatively loosened his legs, and the other warrior rolled onto his back. "I yield," M'Baku said weakly.

T'Challa shakily got to his feet as Zuri approached him. The victor looked at the audience surrounding the Challenge Pool, only moments ago so boisterous, which had now fallen silent.

"Wakanda forever!" He raised his fist to the sky. The crowd erupted in a roar of approval.

Zuri took his place by T'Challa's side, held his other hand high, and proclaimed: "I give you King T'Challa, the Black Panther!"

The entire arena exploded with sound as the nation rejoiced in the new king's victory.

T'Challa looked back to M'Baku as he sulked off through the mouth of the cave entrance from which he had come, trailed by his fellow Jabari tribesmen. They did not congratulate T'Challa on his well-earned victory.

But the new king ignored the insult and turned his attention back to the rest of the Wakandan citizens. He had more important matters at hand. It was now his job, his right, his destiny to protect, serve, and rule as the king of Wakanda.

CHAPTER 3

That night, T'Challa entered the Hall of Kings, his injuries from the battle bandaged and his spirits high. Zuri was awaiting him, the ceremonial vessel from the Challenge Arena at his side.

Zuri bowed. "My king."

T'Challa returned the bow, a small thrill coursing through him at being addressed as "King."

Zuri picked up the ceremonial vessel. T'Challa knew it was filled with a liquid comprised of the heart-shaped herb mixed with water. The liquid began to glow slightly.

"Lay down," Zuri instructed. T'Challa obeyed, lying prone on the ground as he was buried in dirt.

"You have earned the right to reclaim the power of the Black Panther, as is granted all rulers of Wakanda for centuries past until they deem it fit to pass on to the next generation, as your father did with you." Zuri brought the vessel to T'Challa's lips. "Drink and be restored."

T'Challa drank down the contents without hesitation. Within seconds he began to feel the power pulse through his veins. His heartbeat grew loud in his ears.

"Relax," Zuri instructed. "Your spirit will now leave your body and travel to the Ancestral Plane, as is tradition in the coronation. You will have an audience with the Panthers and kings who have come before. Use this time well, my king."

T'Challa felt the world around him begin to swirl and fade as darkness overtook him.

When T'Challa opened his eyes, he was outside. The stars burned extra bright in the sky above and seemed to move in their orbits. Tall acacia trees surrounded the field he was in, and the grasslands moved gently back and forth in the light breeze. As he rose to his feet, T'Challa could see the glowing yellow eyes of panthers perched in one such particularly majestic tree, their jet-black coats blending in with the night. These were the spirits of the Black Panthers of generations past. Suddenly, one of the panthers leaped down from the tree and transformed into a familiar figure, who began to approach him. Tears immediately welled in T'Challa's eyes.

"Baba," he whispered.

Before him stood the spirit of T'Chaka, dressed in full royal gown. Next to that spirit was a shadow of a younger T'Chaka, wearing his Black Panther suit. The two personages merged as T'Chaka reached his son. T'Challa grabbed his father in a tight hug.

"My son, my king, my Black Panther." T'Chaka smiled proudly. "I never doubted you."

"I did, Baba. Forgive me, but for a moment, in the Challenge Pool, I had a moment of reservation," T'Challa confessed.

"And what eased that doubt?" T'Chaka asked.

"The cries of the people. Of my people. I could not fail in my duty and disappoint them," T'Challa said, remembering his hesitation in the pool, when he was nearly sure M'Baku would overtake him, before the chanting of the Wakandans reached his ears and revived his spirit.

T'Chaka smiled again. "Remember that feeling, my son. You are correct: They are *your* people now, and they will look to you for guidance. The path of a ruler is long and filled with moments where you will question yourself. Do you not think I had my own personal crises, times when I doubted myself or wondered what was best for our land?"

T'Challa was surprised. He had assumed T'Chaka was never anything but the strong figure of a confident leader that T'Challa had always looked up to and admired, even idolized.

"Really?" he asked skeptically.

"Of course," T'Chaka answered. "I surrounded myself with wise advisers, elders, and, of course, your mother. That you never saw my doubts as a ruler is what helped me to be successful and guide you."

"You were taken from us before your time, Baba. I don't know that I am ready." T'Challa looked at his father pleadingly.

His father placed both of his hands on T'Challa's shoulders and looked deep into his son's eyes. "A man who has not prepared his children for his own death has failed as a father. Have I ever failed you, son?"

T'Challa shook his head.

"You must move forward. My time has ended. You are king now," T'Chaka said.

"How do I best lead the tribes, Baba? I want to be a great king, like you were." T'Challa truly felt his father had been the greatest ruler of any land.

T'Chaka met his son's gaze. "You will struggle, my son," he said, his voice tinged with sadness.

"Why?" asked T'Challa.

"Because you are a good man," T'Chaka said with a sigh, "and it is hard for good men to be king."

"You were a good man," T'Challa replied.

T'Chaka nodded. "And I had many struggles because of it. But follow your heart. It is a good one. You will know what is best for your nation deep down, and those who help guide you will see it."

Looking up at the stars winking down on him from

the depths of the inky night, T'Chaka let out a long sigh. He turned his attention back to his son. "Our time draws to an end, my son. Go forth and lead, knowing my spirit is always one with yours. Find strength in the power of the Black Panther. And always hold those you love near to you, for they will forever be looking out for your best needs. As will I."

T'Chaka embraced his son, and a moment later T'Challa felt the world around him begin to spin once more, whirling and blurring until there was only blackness.

When his eyes snapped open again, T'Challa was once more in the Hall of Kings. He turned his gaze to Zuri.

"Send me back. I have more questions," T'Challa begged the shaman.

Zuri shook his head. "You will always have questions. That is what makes a good king."

T'Challa sat up. "I told my father I didn't think I was ready to be king. I am still unsure."

"What is it that troubles you most?" Zuri asked.

"That I failed in keeping my father alive. I told him there was something wrong at the United Nations gathering. I felt it, but I did not act upon it." T'Challa dropped his head at the memory. "Perhaps M'Baku was right. If I couldn't protect my father, my king, then who am I to rule?"

Zuri placed a hand gently on T'Challa's chin and lifted it. "Pay no heed to that mountain dweller. He knows nothing of what he spoke. In your heart you know you did what was best. You also know there was nothing you could have said or done to stop your father from speaking that day. It was an important decision, and his to make alone. The consequences do not fall on your shoulders. Shake off that burden and learn to forgive yourself."

"You make that sound so easy," T'Challa said quietly.

"Always keep these words in mind, my king: The world is too unpredictable to know for certain what is to come next. You can only prepare best in anticipation. No one knows what the future holds or where the next threat will come from, not even a king."

T'Challa looked up and saw his father's royal casket nearby. He took in Zuri's words and those his father's spirit had spoken on the Ancestral Plane. Getting to his feet, T'Challa walked to his father's casket, kissed it, and walked out of the hall as Wakanda's newest king.

CHAPTER 4

LONDON, UNITED KINGDOM

It was raining in London.

As usual, the Museum of Great Britain's Director Manning thought with a sigh as she waited in the museum cafeteria line for her morning tea. When it was her turn to order, she approached the counter and noticed a new face ready to serve her.

"Good morning." She looked at the barista, who she didn't recognize. "First day on the job?"

"Yes, ma'am," the barista answered. She was American, Director Manning noted.

"Welcome. I'll have a tea, black, milk and sugar please." As the barista worked on her order, Director Manning looked around. The museum was already bustling with activity. Tourists, regular patrons, and a group of school-children on a field trip all milled about the entryway and made their way from one exhibit hall to another. It would be a busy day, she thought.

"Here you are, ma'am." The barista's voice broke into her reverie.

The director fetched the cup from the young woman's hand and took a sip. "Wonderful, thank you." She smiled at the new barista. "Welcome to the museum."

She turned away and took another sip as she began to make her way to her office.

"Director," a voice called out from her left. It belonged to an approaching security guard.

"Yes?" she answered.

"There is a gent in the West African Wing requesting to meet with you," he said.

Director Manning furrowed her brow. Museumgoers were not usually predisposed to requesting the director's presence to offer feedback on specific exhibits. "What seems to be the problem?" she asked.

The guard hesitated, "No problem, ma'am—it's just, he's looking at the items like he's in a bloody shopping mall or something."

"Very well, Edmund, thank you. I'll see myself there." The director walked toward the West African Wing, the sound of her high heels clicking on the parquet floor.

As she entered the wing, she saw a tall, dark-skinned man dressed in very fashionable and very expensive-looking street wear in the back corner of the exhibit. He wore a large gold chain around his neck and cut an imposing figure. As the security guard had noted, he was observing the artifacts closely, as though he were picking out a gift.

"Hello there. I am Director Manning. You wished to see me?" She extended her hand to shake his. The man ignored it. Instead, he pointed at an African tribal mask hanging on the wall.

"Tell me about this one. What do you know?" the man asked abruptly.

She examined the mask, taken aback by his curtness.

"A ninth-century shaman tribal mask from the Benin region. We believe it was used in burial rituals."

"And this?" He pointed to an ax, crumbled and dull with age, but well-preserved.

"A building ax from the eleventh century, Tangier region. Used for chopping wood to help in making roofs for huts," the director answered.

The man stepped in front of what appeared to be a mining tool and paused. He looked at the item with particular interest. If the director didn't know better, she would have sworn he looked like a child at his birthday party and everything behind the glass was his celebratory bounty.

Without prompting, she began to describe the item. "Seventh century, a mining hammer, also from Benin, belonging to the Fula Tribe, it was—"

"Nah," the man cut her off.

"I beg your pardon?" The director's tone was cold. She was getting annoyed.

The man finally extended his hand. She tentatively shook it, noting his strong grip. "Erik Killmonger," the man introduced himself at last. "You know your stuff, I gotta hand it to ya. But this?" He pointed to the hammer.

"Yeah, it was taken by British soldiers in Benin, but it's not from there, and it's definitely not seventh century."

He turned back to face her and smiled in a way that made the director quite uncomfortable. "That hammer is from Wakanda, over two thousand years old, and made of pure vibranium. Don't worry if you haven't heard of that place or don't have any other items from the region; they're pretty famous for being possessive."

"I—I…" the director stammered as Killmonger's face grew dark.

"I'mma tell you what. I'll just go ahead and take it off your hands. I think you've had it long enough," he said, a menacing grin slowly breaking out over his features.

Before she could protest, Director Manning felt a sharp pain in her stomach. Grabbing her midsection, she suddenly collapsed to the ground, unconscious.

Killmonger laughed. "You Brits will trust anything as long as it tastes like tea." Looking around, he called out to the few visitors farther down the wing. "Yo, we need a medic over here!"

Within seconds two EMTs rushed in with a stretcher and asked everyone to calmly evacuate the exhibit.

Museum patrons cautiously backed out as the EMTs roped off the area. They then turned their attention to the fallen director.

"She doesn't look too good, does she, Limbani?" one of the EMTs mused to the other. "Must be something in the water."

"That's what I'm thinking, Klaue," replied the other man.

These were not EMTs. The first man was Ulysses Klaue, international thief and terrorist. He and his associate, Limbani, were wanted across the globe for over a dozen crimes, including a massive bombing in Wakanda that resulted in the loss of multiple lives and the theft of three hundred pounds of pure Vibranium. They'd now teamed up with Erik Killmonger.

Turning to Killmonger, Klaue removed his gloves. "Let's see if you know what you're talking about, shall we?" He looked down at his hand. It was a bionic prosthetic, Klaue having lost his original hand to Ultron before the android's recent defeat by the Avengers.

Before he could do anything, two security guards stormed the entrance of the exhibit. "Oi! Do you need assistance? What's happened to Director Manning?" one of them asked.

Klaue turned to face the man. "She'll be fine. I think. We're just doing a bit of browsing, but we've found what we need here, right? Great customer service, though. You won't be needed anymore."

With that, he raised his hand and aimed it at the men. A sonic pulse fired from his hand, knocking the security guards back. Limbani crouched down to examine them. "Out cold," he pronounced.

Klaue turned his attention back to the display case, raised his hand, and fired another pulse. It shattered the glass into millions of pieces but left the contents within unharmed. He walked over and removed the "mining tool" Killmonger had claimed was Wakandan. As he held it in his hand, his bionic limb began to vibrate and sizzle. Slowly, centuries of caked dirt and debris began to fall off the artifact.

After a few moments, the "mining tool" resting in Klaue's hand was revealed, indeed, to be a hammer of pure, shining vibranium.

"*Oooh-hoo!* What did I tell you?" Killmonger hooted, his eyes alight at seeing his conviction validated.

"We're going to make a fortune on this. Good job, Killmonger," Klaue said, a smile stretched across his face.

"Trying to sell pure vibranium on the black market? Good luck." Killmonger gave a slight chuckle.

"Already have a buyer in place. Don't take me for an amateur," Klaue retorted.

"Hope you know what you're doing. Once word leaks this is out there, you'll have Wakandans all over your butt. They don't take to stealing," Killmonger warned.

Klaue raised his bionic hand and put it in Killmonger's face. "Again, not my first time dealing with Wakandans. Or vibranium. You did a good job leading us here, now let's wrap this up so I can move on to the next phase."

Killmonger nodded in salute. "You're the boss." He walked over to the stretcher and lay down in the bag that rested on top of it. Klaue placed the vibranium hammer on Killmonger's chest, and Limbani quickly zipped up the bag, sealing both Killmonger and the hammer inside.

Klaue and Limbani lifted the stretcher and hurried out through the museum's emergency exit. Outside, an ambulance waited for them. They quickly loaded Killmonger's stretcher in the back, and Klaue hopped in behind, closing the doors. Limbani climbed in the passenger's seat.

He turned to the driver: It was the barista from the museum cafeteria.

"Great job. Just remind me never to order a drink from you." He laughed.

"Okay, scram time," Klaue said as the barista started the engine. "Let's go make it rain," he said, unzipping the bag so Killmonger could climb out. Klaue reached for the vibranium hammer and turned it over in his hands, a gleeful look in his eye.

The barista revved the engine and turned on the siren, and the criminals pulled away from the museum and into the bustling London streets. Moments later another ambulance raced onto the scene, and this time real EMTs exited, running toward the museum doors with an empty stretcher, unaware of the heist that had just happened.

CHAPTER 5

The warm Wakandan breeze carried with it the smells and sounds of the area surrounding the Royal Palace. Nakia and T'Challa walked along the streets of Step Town, an up-and-coming neighborhood in Wakanda filled with artists and entrepreneurs, likely the leaders of the next generation. Everywhere one looked there was creativity, ideas and inspiration being born. T'Challa liked to visit Step Town whenever he needed a break from life at the center of the Royal Palace, when he needed to feel grounded.

Now he drew in a deep breath. "The scent of home."

Nakia nodded appreciatively. "Home. And now your realm, my king," she said, a teasing spark in her eye.

"I was talking about you," he said, sneaking a sideways glance in time to see Nakia blush. "And I may be Wakanda's king, but to you I hope I am something more."

Nakia smiled, a memory from their childhood flooding her brain. "A thief."

T'Challa was confused. "What did I ever...? *Ohhhh.*"

"A royal security hover bike," they said in unison.

"I was ten. I hardly think that qualifies me as a career criminal." T'Challa laughed. "And if you'll recall, *you* were the one trying to steal it."

"And *you* lifted the Kimoyo beads off the royal guard." Nakia smiled back. "So you were an accessory, at the very least."

"We rode through the city until sundown. It was a long summer day; we didn't return to the palace until past dinner." T'Challa's gaze appeared far away as he remembered every detail. "You rode without fear."

"Which is less than I can say for you when we got back and you had to face your father. You were terrified." Nakia laughed.

"Baba was angry, yes, but mainly concerned for my safety. And yours. He sent me to my room without dinner."

"You never told me he punished you for it," Nakia said, surprised.

T'Challa smiled. "I never considered it a punishment. It gave me time to think and to come to a conclusion. That was the day I decided I wanted to be with you for the rest of my life. Even if it cost me supper."

The king looked into Nakia's eyes, searching for evidence that she felt similarly. But Nakia dropped her head and turned to watch a street performer turning and whirling with ease to a beat only he could hear.

Nakia sighed. "I want to be back out in the field, T'Challa."

"Always the free spirit." T'Challa tried to hide his hurt at Nakia's apparent rejection, his jesting tone belying his true feelings.

"I'm serious. I have spent the past two years in Nigeria. What you saw the other day in Chibok was just a fraction of the work I've been doing. There is far more to be done for those women." Nakia turned to face T'Challa. "Unless we can liberate them by granting them sanctuary here."

"Allowing outsiders across our borders is a violation of one of our oldest rules," T'Challa responded sharply.

"Look what happened when my father extended his hand to the outside world. It cost him his life."

Nakia pressed onward, undeterred by T'Challa's tone. "And there are women and children losing their lives every day to the militants. I can't stand behind closed borders in a hidden nation and ignore what they are going through. I'm sorry, T'Challa. It's my calling."

T'Challa looked at the woman he loved—who he wasn't certain loved him back—her face set in determination. As he saw the passion in her eyes to save outsiders, he couldn't help but fall a little more in love with her. He also knew he could not deny her request, keeping her in Wakanda simply because he wanted her close.

"Fine," the Wakandan king conceded. "I'll alert the other War Dogs that you will be going back out into the world. But on a new mission this time."

Nakia was confused. "What 'new mission'? I thought we just agreed I'd return to my work."

"You said you wanted to go out into the field. I hear there is work that can be done in a beautiful place like Hawaii." T'Challa looked at her for a moment before his face broke into a grin. "I'll even join you."

She shook her head. "You're not going to make this easy on me, are you?" Nakia asked, smiling.

"Have I ever? And now I'm king." T'Challa crossed his arms and faked a "serious" face.

"No matter. I can always steal another hover bike. I'm an independent woman now, who doesn't need a prince as her accomplice." She poked him in the chest.

"You are certainly your own woman, Nakia. Of that, there is no denying," T'Challa said. The street performer's dance ended, and the small crowd that had gathered broke into enthusiastic applause.

T'Challa joined in, thinking of the last time he'd heard applause—at the Challenge Pool, when he'd beaten M'Baku. The moment he'd agreed to govern an entire nation, a thought that led him to remember his father's words to him on the Ancestral Plane: He would need help.

The grass grew tall in the plains of Wakanda, enough so that a man could take root there almost undetected, invisible.

Unless, of course, that man was feeding a two-ton rhinoceros, which was exactly what W'Kabi, another of T'Challa's childhood compatriots, was doing as T'Challa approached him. W'Kabi, always levelheaded and honest, was someone to whom T'Challa had gone for advice throughout their many years of friendship. W'Kabi knew T'Challa better than anyone, save possibly Ramonda and Nakia.

"Is it possible that M20 can grow any more before he explodes? You spoil him, my friend," T'Challa said, admiring the larger-than-life animal placidly grazing on the treats his doting master had set out before him. "I remember when you found him, orphaned, barely able to stand on his own."

"Children ask to ride him every day. We have a fearless generation growing in these lands." W'Kabi flashed a smile at his oldest, closest friend. "I believe they are taking after their king."

"Will I ever get used to hearing that title and not look to see if my father is behind me?" T'Challa asked, only half joking.

"You are sure to grow into it." W'Kabi gave the rhino

a pat on the rump and left him to his meal as the two friends began to stroll through the fields. "I noticed Nakia has returned."

"Not for long, if she has her way." T'Challa's voice was tinged with sadness.

W'Kabi chuckled. "Which means 'not for long, period.' We both know Nakia always gets her way."

T'Challa looked at his best friend. "Aside from Nakia, no one knows me better than you. And few know Wakanda as well as you." He sighed. "You might even have more of a sense of these lands than I do."

"What troubles your mind, my king?" W'Kabi sensed this was more than just a social call.

"There was a ritual I went through after the Challenge Pool. Thanks to Zuri and the heart-shaped herb, I had the chance to see my father once more, to speak with him," T'Challa confided. "One of the lessons he taught me in order to become a good ruler was to surround myself with people I can trust, people who know me and whose counsel I can seek. The tribal elders see me as an adventurer, young and untested in the ways of politics. They need to see me with someone they respect: a warrior and one of

Wakanda's most faithful and hardworking citizens. Not to mention one of the greatest strategic minds I've ever known. To be honest, I need someone at my side whom I trust as well."

Sensing where this was leading, W'Kabi sought to focus T'Challa's thoughts. "Is there a reason you are bringing this to my attention, my friend?"

T'Challa stopped walking and gripped W'Kabi's shoulder. "I need a royal adviser. I am hoping you are willing and up to the task?"

"It would be my honor to serve you," W'Kabi answered immediately, gripping T'Challa's shoulder in a return gesture of affection. The lifelong friends hugged. Pulling out of the embrace, W'Kabi smirked playfully. "My first piece of advice: no chasing Avengers in broad daylight in full Panther garb."

As the men laughed, W'Kabi couldn't help but notice there seemed to be something more on T'Challa's mind.

"In order to advise you, I need to know what still troubles you. So, my king, what is it?" asked the newly appointed royal adviser.

T'Challa shook his head ruefully. "Nakia. She said

something that I can't shake. She wants to do more for the oppressed she is helping to free in her work for the outside world. She believes Wakanda could be of service as a haven to refugees who no longer have homes to return to."

W'Kabi was taken aback. "My king, you do realize what Nakia is suggesting? It's dangerous. When we start letting people in, their problems become our problems. Soon, Wakanda would become like every other nation."

T'Challa seemed to be reconsidering his earlier position. "But if we have the resources to help—"

A flash of light emitted from the pair's Kimoyo bracelets as suddenly a hologram of Okoye's face projected from the beads into the field. "Sorry to interrupt, Your Highness, but guess who just popped back up on our radar? Ulysses Klaue has resurfaced."

T'Challa felt his stomach drop. Ulysses Klaue was a sworn enemy of Wakanda, a perpetual threat who had made it his mission to steal Wakanda's Vibranium and exploit the invaluable natural resource for his own selfish gain. Anywhere Klaue popped up, suffering and trauma were sure to follow.

"Gather everyone to the Tribal Council Room

immediately. We are on our way." T'Challa turned to W'Kabi. "A discussion to continue later. Now, I feel, will come the first trial by fire, for both of us."

The pair ran through the fields en route to the Royal Palace.

A little while later, Okoye was in front of T'Challa, Ramonda, W'Kabi, and the tribal elders, recounting the theft of the vibranium hammer from the Museum of Great Britain, using street cams as well as security footage from inside the exhibit.

"It was a clean getaway, exquisitely timed. Klaue had this planned perfectly," she concluded.

"And is likely to sell the hammer to the highest bidder, if history has shown us anything," T'Challa said gravely.

Okoye nodded. "We have received intel that there is already an interested party. In fact, we've tracked his location and where the buy is scheduled to transpire: Busan, South Korea. A hub of deep black market dealings go down there."

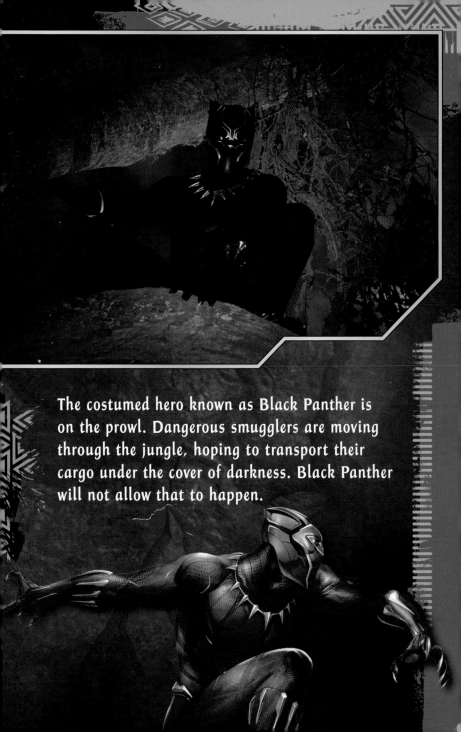

The costumed hero known as Black Panther is on the prowl. Dangerous smugglers are moving through the jungle, hoping to transport their cargo under the cover of darkness. Black Panther will not allow that to happen.

With the help of incredibly high-tech gadgets and a suit interwoven with rare and impervious vibranium, Black Panther is able to take down the criminals without any casualties. He removes his fearsome helmet to reveal he is T'Challa, future king of Wakanda.

After convincing his childhood friend Nakia to join him, T'Challa boards their futuristic ride to the self-isolated but extremely technologically advanced nation that he is bound to rule as warrior-king.

Safely home, T'Challa greets his mother, the queen, Ramonda. Since the death of T'Challa's father, T'Chaka, and T'Challa's fight with the Avengers, Ramonda has been worried about her son—but she is also proud of the man he's become.

Most of the clans in Wakanda are happy with the Black Panther clan's rule, and they concede the throne. M'Baku, leader of the Jabari clan from the mountains, is not. He will confront T'Challa.

T'Challa prepares to battle the much larger warrior without his Black Panther gear—and stripped of the super strength and speed that he is normally granted.

The High Shaman Zuri, T'Challa's good friend, watches the struggle unfold. He is a font of wisdom about Wakanda and its customs.

Nakia, Okoye, and Ayo, a member of the Dora Milaje, also watch the two warriors anxiously. The Dora Milaje are the royal guard of Wakanda and are among the best fighting forces in the world.

After a brutal fight, T'Challa is victorious! He prepares himself physically and spiritually to assume his throne as king of Wakanda and the protector of his nation—the Black Panther.

But the peace his victory has brought to Wakanda is short-lived. International terrorist and thief Ulysses Klaue has resurfaced and has nefarious plans to steal precious vibranium.

This is not an attack that T'Challa takes lightly. He gathers his most trusted warriors and prepares to intercept Klaue at an illegal casino in Busan, South Korea.

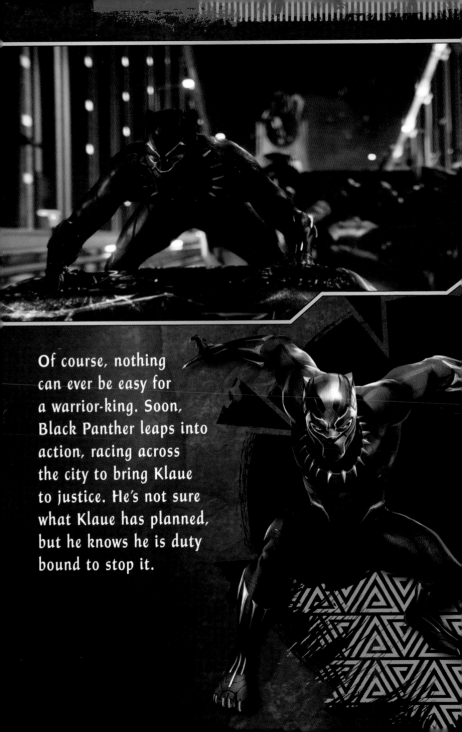

Of course, nothing can ever be easy for a warrior-king. Soon, Black Panther leaps into action, racing across the city to bring Klaue to justice. He's not sure what Klaue has planned, but he knows he is duty bound to stop it.

"Then that is where I shall capture him," T'Challa stated matter-of-factly.

Instantly, the room echoed with protests. "You were only just crowned king," said the Mining Tribe Elder. "Your place is here."

"Do you not think this is a job better suited for the Dora Milaje?" asked Ramonda gently.

But T'Challa would not be swayed. "Klaue has been the only person to have ever successfully invaded Wakanda and stolen its vibranium. He then used the stolen vibranium to assist Ultron, who laid waste to Sokovia. His heist cost dozens of Wakandan lives in the bombing that covered his escape." T'Challa became impassioned as he spoke, even as his tone remained measured and even. "Not capturing Klaue over the past thirty years was one of my father's only regrets."

The tribal elders all looked around wordlessly, acknowledging their king had raised valid points.

"Wakanda needs their king *and* the Black Panther to finally bring Klaue to justice." T'Challa looked to W'Kabi for his input.

"King T'Challa is right," W'Kabi agreed. "He and

a small team of Dora Milaje are best suited for this operation."

The room muttered their acceptance, not completely pleased, but understanding the importance of the task.

"I only wish I could go with you," W'Kabi said to T'Challa, pulling him aside after the meeting had disbanded. Okoye joined the pair.

"I think the princess Shuri has some things for our king that could help, and ease your mind, W'Kabi. She asked me to bring you to her labs as soon as the meeting was over," Okoye said to T'Challa.

"She was anticipating my joining the mission?" T'Challa asked.

"Never a doubt. She was counting on it." Okoye smiled. She and T'Challa bade W'Kabi good-bye, exited the Tribal Council Room, and headed to meet Shuri for some accoutrements that would guarantee T'Challa's success against Klaue.

CHAPTER 6

T'Challa flew toward Mount Bashenga, also known as the Great Mound. It was the major natural source of Wakanda's vibranium. A large cliff face was on one side, dropping off steeply; the other was littered with sloping hills. At the top stood an impressive laboratory that seemed to be built from the ground itself, incorporating the vibranium deposits there into its architecture. This was the home of the Wakandan Design Group.

Once inside the Design Group's building, T'Challa could not help but look around in awe. Despite having visited countless times, he never failed to marvel at the technological achievements and breakthroughs the group seemed to make daily. Hearing a familiar voice dictating to lab techs and interns on multiple assignments at once, he smiled.

"Where are we on the RTF antigrav shielding? Make sure Kimoyo updates are on track. I need to see the specs for the new hover train—the Royal City's planning committee wants an update." In the midst of all the chaos and energy, Shuri appeared at home, comfortable, and in charge as she dictated commands and instructions to the other lab designers.

Dressed in a lab coat, her hair held back with multiple pens, the princess-turned-high-tech-genius didn't even glance up from her clipboard as T'Challa entered. "I've already sent a vibranium-laced car to Busan. It will be there when you arrive. Here." She handed T'Challa a vibranium disc. "This will allow me to interface remotely with whatever you attach the disc to. Use it if you get separated and need another ride. I'm assuming Okoye will be joining you?"

T'Challa nodded and cleared his throat. "And Nakia."

Shuri's eyebrows shot up. "Nakia?"

"It's a three-person mission," T'Challa countered, coming across more defensive than he'd intended.

Shuri smiled knowingly. "Whatever you say, brother." Choosing not to press him any further, she nodded toward the table. It was covered in black sand that seemed more like liquid as it moved in waves over the surface. T'Challa recognized them as vibranium nanites.

"You prepare us well, sister," T'Challa said admiringly. "And, yes, I will be recruiting Nakia to join us. She *did* want to get back in the field, after all. And I know how much you like to show off your talents." T'Challa winked at his sister.

"Please," Shuri scoffed. "That's nothing. Wait until you see what I've done with your Panther outfit."

T'Challa stopped short. "My suit?"

"The very one," Shuri replied as she walked over to two mannequins positioned next to each other. One was dressed in the traditional Black Panther uniform, the other was bare, save for a necklace around its neck that featured a ceremonial panther tooth.

"Overhaul? I like my suit," T'Challa protested.

Shuri laughed. "Oh, it's great, don't get me wrong, as long as you can get the bad guys to stop shooting at you while you say, *Hold on, let me put on my helmet, cool?*"

"So what is the necklace?" T'Challa asked, brushing off his sister's sarcasm.

"*That* is your suit." Shuri beamed.

"I liked my chances better with a helmet," T'Challa remarked dryly.

"Brother, you are so gonna eat those words." Shuri was practically jumping up and down with excitement. "Okay, now look at the necklace and activate it."

"Activate it? How?" T'Challa was used to his sister's brain working faster than her mouth, but he was starting to get frustrated.

"With your mind! Think about the suit forming," Shuri instructed him.

T'Challa gave a wary glance at his sister before focusing his attention on the mannequin with the necklace. He envisioned the suit on the figure instead. Suddenly, millions of vibranium nanites flew out of the necklace, swirling around the mannequin. They quickly formed a sleek new suit of Black Panther body armor around the mannequin, covering it head to toe.

Shuri beamed with pride. "You haven't even seen the

best part!" Turning to T'Challa, she moved him closer to the new suit. "Now, kick it."

Without hesitation, T'Challa gave the suit a round-house kick that landed solidly in the square of the chest. The mannequin flew back against the wall. Picking it up, Shuri pointed to where his foot had made contact. The area was now softly glowing blue.

"The nanites absorb kinetic energy and hold it for redistribution. Now, hit it again." She took out a small camera and began filming.

T'Challa gave another swift kick to the same place on the suit. A small flash of energy discharged, and the Wakandan king went flying backward. The suit remained exactly in place.

"Amazing, right?!" Shuri giggled as she filmed T'Challa climbing back to his feet.

"Delete that footage," he said, not amused.

"Is that how you thank your brilliant sister? Now, suit up—or necklace on or whatever. You have a bad guy to catch. I'm gonna show Mom." Shuri was still chuckling as she gathered her things.

T'Challa looked at the suit, imagined it in its necklace form again, and the nanites detached themselves. In a flurry, they re-formed into the panther-tooth necklace. He lifted it off the mannequin and put it around his neck.

"You're good," he said admiringly.

"We'll see how good it is once it's in the field," Shuri replied. "Come on, brother. I have more to show you before you leave." The pair turned and exited the lab.

The Jagalchi Fish Market in Busan, South Korea, was as active and loud at night as it was during the day. Vendors were still stationed at their stalls, selling the day's catch. People crowded the streets as they made their way through tight corridors of tents and buildings.

Okoye parked the car Shuri had promised them by the side of a building. She exited, tugging at the wig that covered her tattooed head. "Can we get in and out quickly so I can remove this cursed thing and never wear it again?"

Nakia and T'Challa climbed out of the car. "That's one of the reasons I agreed to join you two, to help get this done," Nakia said as she made her way to an elderly woman selling fish. The two exchanged pleasantries in Korean as Nakia motioned to Okoye and T'Challa. The king was in a sharply tailored suit, his panther-tooth necklace on, while both women were clad in gorgeous evening gowns. They definitely looked out of place in a fish market.

"So far no eyes on Klaue," Okoye said, looking around.

"And Nakia seems to have made a friend," T'Challa remarked with a smile, as Nakia rejoined them from where she'd been conferencing with the elderly woman.

"A contact of mine. This is the place," she reported.

T'Challa looked impressed. "That's a contact?"

"What can I say? I know the right people. Now let's get inside." She nodded at the two bulky figures guarding the back door to the building they had parked near.

The trio walked over to the door, and the beefier of the two guards held out an arm to stop them. "Weapons," he said shortly.

T'Challa shot Nakia an inquisitive glance, but she just nodded at him, urging him along. T'Challa, Nakia, and Okoye dropped their weapons at the feet of the guard. They were then ushered through a metal detector to ensure they weren't concealing any more weaponry. Finally, they were escorted through the entrance by the two guards and deposited in a large room filled with sounds and lights. There were people everywhere, all dressed to the nines.

And all had one thing on their mind: winning.

They had entered an underground casino. It was a veritable hub of activity, two stories tall with a wraparound balcony overlooking the main casino floor. Lounge areas were nestled in nooks to the sides. Every casino game imaginable was represented; the floor was filled with high rollers playing for big stakes.

"Klaue certainly didn't pick this place for a quiet exchange. There's no telling where he could be," Okoye said, taking in the room.

Nakia motioned to the cashier's cage. "Everyone exchange money for some *won* and hit the tables. There's nothing more suspicious in a casino than three people standing around not gambling."

They exchanged some of their notes and bills into Korean money and split up, assuming various vantage points around the floor.

"No sign of Klaue or his associates," Okoye said into her comm. Nakia adjusted her earpiece and looked around.

"No, but we do have company. I spot three . . . wait, five Americans," she said. "From the looks of it, they might be our buyers."

T'Challa caught a glimpse of one of the men Nakia referred to seated at a blackjack table. T'Challa's brow furrowed. "They are. And they're not any ordinary Americans," he said, making his way over to the table.

Taking a seat next to the American, T'Challa placed money down for his bet as the dealer shuffled a new deck of cards. T'Challa glanced sideways at the man and said casually, "So, Special Agent Everett Ross, tell me, what is the CIA doing in a South Korean illegal casino?"

Agent Ross jumped slightly but quickly recovered, giving T'Challa a sidelong glance. "I imagine we're here for the same reason the Wakandan king is," he answered, matching the nonchalance in T'Challa's voice. "The tables here are hot." The men kept their voices low so as not to attract attention.

"They will only get hotter once a certain villain arrives, carrying property of Wakanda," T'Challa answered.

"Oh, where are my manners? Congratulations are in order. How's the crown fit?" Ross asked.

"Do not dodge me, Ross. I am leaving here with Klaue. He's a very wanted man where I come from." T'Challa's face brooked no room for argument.

Ross nodded toward the table. "Blackjack. You're on a roll these days. But the table's the only place where you're bound to catch a win tonight, T'Challa. What I'm doing or not doing here on behalf of the United States' government is none of your concern. Whatever you're here to do, just do me a favor and wait until I've done what *I* need to do."

T'Challa glowered. "I gave you Zemo."

"And I kept it under wraps that the king of a Third-World country runs around in a bulletproof catsuit. We're even." Ross turned to the dealer. "I think my friend is just gonna let it ride, so keep dealing."

T'Challa leaned in close to Ross and said in a near growl, "Make no mistake, Klaue is leaving with me. You have been warned." With that, he got up from the table and made his way to a lounge area.

The dealer dealt the departing king another hit. Ross turned to her. "I'll just hold on to these for my lucky friend," he said with a smile. Turning, he spoke into a comm mic in his sleeve. "Ross to all agents, the king of Wakanda is in the house. Do not let him leave with the target. Copy?" The five agents radioed that they had copied as Everett Ross made eye contact with T'Challa across the room; T'Challa was still staring at him coldly. Ross raised his drink, nodded to the king, and took a deep gulp of the amber liquid. They both knew the night had just become a lot more complicated.

"I see you're making friends," Okoye said to T'Challa through their own comm devices.

"And leaving behind a ton of money," Nakia chimed in.

"The Americans are CIA." T'Challa sipped a drink in the lounge area as he watched Ross get up to move to another table, taking T'Challa's winnings with him.

"So we heard," said Nakia.

"Will this be a problem?" Okoye asked.

T'Challa stood. "As long as Ross minds his place and knows what is best for him, we shall leave with what we came for." His voice was steel. He began to walk toward

Ross, hoping to catch the agent before he could settle at another table.

"Didn't we just do this dance, Your Highness?" Ross asked as T'Challa blocked his path. "Unless you want your money. Don't worry," he said, patting a briefcase, "I brought my own. But I don't think you were planning on buying the item in question, were you?"

T'Challa pushed the agent's fistful of Korean money aside. "Nothing should buy the price of freedom for a known terrorist."

Ross sighed. "You think I care about the vibranium? I wouldn't have three of my best men with me if I was just going on a shopping spree."

"Five of your men," T'Challa corrected him.

Agent Ross raised his eyebrow. "You've already made them all? I'm impressed. I would expect no less from the Black Panther, though."

"I am prepared to bring in Klaue no matter what it takes," T'Challa stated.

"That makes two of us. But if the catsuit makes another appearance, I may have to bring you both in. Don't make me do something we'll both regret," Ross countered.

"Cross me and you *will* regret it, Ross." T'Challa stared the man down.

"We're not gonna play *rock, paper, panther* for custody of Klaue, so tell your two lovely bodyguards they should stand down as well." Ross smiled at T'Challa's look of surprise. "Yeah, I made your crew, too."

T'Challa crossed his arms. "Do not make an enemy of me this night, Ross. Klaue is the worst threat Wakanda has ever faced. I have the chance to end that, tonight. I'm not letting him get away."

Nakia's voice came through T'Challa's earpiece. "Can you two call a truce or something? You're starting to attract attention."

"The United States government has heard you and respectfully declines, King T'Challa." Ross flashed T'Challa a forced grin. "But I don't think you're going to let that stop you, so—may the best man win."

CHAPTER 8

In the meantime, outside the casino, four heavily armored black SUVs pulled up to the door. Ulysses Klaue and eight men in his security detail exited the vehicles. They walked past the Korean bodyguard and entered the building.

The sudden entrance of such a large entourage quickly grabbed Okoye's attention as Klaue and his men sauntered through and took their positions in the casino.

"Klaue plus eight," she said into her comm, and swiftly made her way up to the balcony from the ground floor. The higher ground enabled her to track more of the men simultaneously.

"He's here. Scat," Ross said to T'Challa.

"We're evenly matched if we team up against him," T'Challa countered.

"You're not getting him that easily. My boys can handle him. Now go, before you blow the entire operation."

Ross quickly settled himself at a nearby poker table and looked around. T'Challa had vanished. Ross was impressed and, if he was being honest, mildly surprised.

"Do you have eyes on the vibranium, Okoye?" T'Challa asked as he made his way to a craps table within sight of Ross.

"Negative, Your Highness. But his men are fanning out across the casino," she answered.

"Yeah, and heavily armed. They're not even bothering to conceal their guns. I thought this was a no-weapons-allowed establishment," Nakia remarked.

Okoye patted the short spear strapped to her thigh. "They're not the only ones armed."

T'Challa reached for his necklace. "Indeed."

Across the floor, Klaue took a seat next to Agent Ross at the poker table. "Quite the posse. Got a new album dropping soon?" Ross quipped.

"Yeah, I'll be sure to get you a copy. Throw it in free

with today's purchase," Klaue answered without missing a beat. "You have the diamonds?"

Ross pulled out his briefcase. "As per our agreement."

Klaue reached into his jacket, pulled out a brown paper bag, and set it on the table. The word *fragile* was written on it in black marker. "I looked everywhere but couldn't find a gift shop with the right wrapping paper that said *rare priceless metal inside.* Hope this'll do."

"As long as it's got what you promised. But it's the thought that counts," Ross replied.

"T'Challa..." Nakia's voice was tense.

"I see it." T'Challa moved closer to the table.

Okoye radioed in: "I do not advise engaging. There are too many guns in this cramped space. I say we take our chances with the CIA and catch up to Klaue's men outside."

T'Challa shook his head. "No. We risk losing both if we act after Klaue has handed over the vibranium."

"So what's your play, party crasher?" Nakia asked. They were running out of time.

Okoye stepped aside as one of Klaue's men elbowed past her. She ducked her head but could tell she had been made. The man stopped and turned, following her and motioning to one of his associates, who moved to corner the warrior woman.

"We may have run out of options, I'm afraid," Okoye warned.

As if on cue, the bodyguard tailing her radioed into his own mic. "Wakandans. They're here!"

"At least I can finally lose this," Okoye muttered as she whipped off her wig and pulled out her spear. In one quick movement, she ducked a punch the large bodyguard threw and, using his momentum, propelled him over the railing of the balcony.

The man flew through the air and crashed down onto the table next to Klaue and Agent Ross.

"*Tsk-tsk*. You broke the rules." Klaue wagged his finger at Ross. "No outsiders."

"Oh, trust me, they aren't with us," Ross answered.

A roar came from across the way. "Klaue!" T'Challa thundered as he began to make his way through the now-panicked crowd toward Klaue and the vibranium hammer.

"Joy. They sent their king. Sorry about your dad. Hope

Wakanda has another king ready to take your place," Klaue called to T'Challa as he pocketed the brown paper bag. Turning to Ross, he looked at the man admonishingly. "PS, deal's off."

T'Challa flipped and dodged his way up and over tables, racing to reach Klaue, but the man took off before T'Challa could get to him. Ross looked furious.

"I warned you about turning this mission sideways," he fumed.

T'Challa answered by shoving the man to the ground just as Klaue turned back and opened fire at the pair. The Wakandan king ducked for cover.

Ross looked at the chaos that had erupted on the floor and in the balconies. Apparently, his men had also been made by Klaue's guards and were engaged in combat. "This is all your fault, you realize," Ross scolded T'Challa.

"The fiend shall not escape," T'Challa replied, seeing Nakia and Okoye each fighting Klaue's men as well. Klaue stood in the middle of the mass hysteria surrounding him, smiling. He was actually enjoying this.

Raising his arms, Klaue bellowed to his men, "Light it up!"

T'Challa grabbed Ross and threw him behind the poker table before tipping it over and using it as a shield between the two men and Klaue at just the right moment. Klaue turned and opened fire, the bullets pinging off the table.

"I can't get a shot from here," yelled Ross, his own gun now drawn.

T'Challa glanced around the room. Gunfire sprayed everywhere as innocent bystanders searched for cover or ran for the door. He knew Ross was right: They were outgunned and trapped.

Even worse, it seemed as though Klaue would slip through his fingers as Klaue had once slipped through T'Chaka's.

CHAPTER 9

Man down! Man down!"

The voice of the CIA operative came crackling through Ross's comm. Klaue's bodyguards were overwhelming his men, knocking them out, and tossing them aside.

"I'm almost out of backup. How's your team?" Ross asked T'Challa, both still pinned behind the poker table as Klaue continued to fire at them.

Looking above, T'Challa saw his two most trusted comrades honoring their reputations, valiantly holding their own against Klaue's men.

"They should make up for your losses," he said reassuringly.

Above, Nakia engaged in hand-to-hand combat with one of Klaue's men. She radioed in to Okoye and T'Challa. "Can we wrap this party before any innocents get injured?"

"Doing my best," Okoye answered, hitting a thug in the leg with her spear and then delivering a knockout blow to his face. "Need a hand?"

"I think the king might," Nakia answered, looking down to see T'Challa trapped.

T'Challa signaled them off. "You two handle the guards. Leave Klaue to me." He turned to Ross. "When I say *go*, roll away from this table and try to take out some of Klaue's men."

"What are you going to do?" Ross asked.

T'Challa, sensing his opening, answered by shoving Ross to the side and yelling, "Go!" As Agent Ross rolled sideways, T'Challa leaped high into the air, over the table, lunging in Klaue's direction.

Klaue fired at and missed the soaring Wakandan king, who suddenly landed in front of him. He pointed his weapon directly at T'Challa, mere feet from him now.

"They make kings bulletproof now?" He sneered.

Klaue pulled the trigger...and nothing happened. He was out of ammunition.

"You would be needing bullets to find that out, thief." T'Challa took a step toward Klaue and knocked the gun out of the villain's hand with a swipe.

Klaue smiled. "Hands up?"

"If you wish to make this easier, yes," T'Challa snarled.

"Oh, you misunderstand," Klaue replied. "I meant you."

Klaue's prosthetic hand began to transform in front of T'Challa's eyes into a weapon resembling a large gun.

"Let's see if you go *boom* like Daddy," Klaue said, an evil look in his eye as the sonic disruptor his hand had become began to buzz, priming to fire.

T'Challa barely flipped back behind the poker table to safety when Klaue's sonic disruptor let out a loud noise as it fired in his direction. The blast tore through the table and knocked T'Challa into the dealer's area, dazed and trapped under debris. His eyes fluttered shut as money went flying everywhere.

"Look at that! I made it rain," Klaue crowed. He turned and signaled to his four remaining men. They ran for the door, the bodyguards firing behind them for cover.

Nakia and Okoye saw their prone king buried under piles of wood and brass. Agent Ross was already making his way to T'Challa and motioned for the women to follow Klaue.

"I have T'Challa—don't let Klaue escape!" Ross bellowed.

The two women ran for the exit Klaue and his men had just fled through. They ran down the corridor, the sound of gunfire ahead and then people screaming. As they reached the door to the alley, they saw four SUVs take off into the depths of the fish market.

As Okoye and Nakia raced to their car, Nakia threw a remote Kimoyo bead onto the hood of the car behind them before sliding into the driver's seat. "All yours, Shuri!" she called into her comm as she and Okoye sped away.

"I'm ready." Shuri's voice was steel in Nakia's ear as she stood at attention in front of the black sand table back in the lab. "I also have eyes on the four vehicles that just left your location. I'll send visual to your screen in the car."

Inside the casino, Agent Ross struggled to lift a heavy brass bar off T'Challa. Suddenly, the Wakandan king's eyes snapped open.

"Glad you're still with us. I don't think Wakanda's ready to bury two kings in the span of a couple weeks," Ross said.

"Klaue?" T'Challa asked a bit groggily.

"Your lady friends are in pursuit. Right now, we need to get this off you and see if there's any—"

Ross was cut off by the sound of T'Challa's grunt, followed by a powerful shove that sent the brass beam flying off the king.

"—damage," Ross finished lamely.

T'Challa leaped to his feet, fully recharged. "Klaue will not slip through my grasp again. I swear it on my father's soul." The Wakandan king began to tear off his tattered suit jacket as he made his way to the casino exit.

Meanwhile, Nakia and Okoye were in hot pursuit of the speeding SUVs. "You can't grab any footage to see which one of these Klaue got into, can you, Shuri?" Okoye asked, navigating as Nakia drove, careening around the tight curves of the narrow South Korean streets.

"Nope. Sorry. Underground, illegal casinos don't like having too many cameras for people like me to tap into the feeds," Shuri answered from her lab.

"Looks like we take them out one at a time and hope we get lucky," Nakia said, accelerating even more.

"What of King T'Challa?" Okoye asked.

Nakia smiled. "I am fairly certain he will be joining us soon. I only hope Busan is ready for their first glimpse of a costumed warrior in action."

Black Panther knew he needed to move fast. He raced outside, now fully costumed and ready for action.

"Second car on your right," came a voice in his ear. It was Shuri. Inside her lab, the table transformed again into a holographic image of the car and its surroundings. "Hop on and let me take the wheel."

The car immediately started, the engine revving. Black Panther flipped onto the hood, quickly securing his footing on the car, which sped off in the direction of the fleeing SUVs.

"I'm clearing all the lights in the area so you have greens the entire way," Shuri said, keying code into her tablet with one hand as she "drove" Black Panther's car with the other via swift hand gestures over the holographic image on her table. "You should catch up with Nakia and Okoye in a few moments."

"Find me Klaue," Panther growled.

"Working on it, trust me. Can't you be impressed for one second?" Shuri was beginning to feel the stress as she snapped at her brother.

In their car, Nakia and Okoye gained on the SUVs, which wove in and out of traffic and among one another. "It's like they're playing a shell game," Nakia said.

"They're trying to confuse us in case we figure out which one holds Klaue and the vibranium," Okoye answered.

"Uh-oh," Nakia warned. "Incoming."

One of the drivers had rolled down his window and fired a machine gun back at the women's car. The bullets bounced off the car's exterior, doing no damage.

The driver of the offending SUV turned to the man in the passenger's seat: Klaue. "Their car must be vibranium-laced. We're not gonna shake them by shooting at it."

"Just keep driving to the pickup zone," Klaue ordered. He grabbed a radio and spoke into it. "Limbani, we're ten minutes from the location. What's your status?"

In his helicopter above a beach, Limbani radioed back. "Off the coast in Haeundae. Set to rendezvous at the bridge."

The Haeundae district of Busan was known for its hilly streets that made their way to the beautiful beach. It was one of Busan's wealthiest neighborhoods and a popular place for tourists to go and view the full moon. Klaue hoped that, between the hills and the tourists, he could shake the women tailing him.

As the vehicles entered the Haeundae district, Nakia managed to gain on the SUV, firing at them. Okoye rolled down the window and leaned out, spear in hand.

"A little closer!" she called out to Nakia.

"Don't forget, *you* aren't made of vibranium. Watch out for that gunman!" Nakia swerved to the other side of the vehicle so they were no longer in the driver's line of fire. She floored the gas pedal and inched closer.

"Almost...almost," Okoye muttered under her breath. "There." With a heave, she threw her spear at the back tires of the SUV. It hit the axis and cracked it, flipping the SUV end over end.

Nakia spun the car around and brought it to a halt

next to the SUV, which was on its side. Okoye leaped on top, looked inside, and then let out a groan of frustration. "Just the driver, out cold. No Klaue."

"Next one, then! Back in, they're getting away," Nakia called out.

Suddenly, the two women saw a car speed by. They were surprised to see Black Panther "surfing" on the hood and no one in the driver's seat.

"He sure knows how to make an entrance," Nakia said. Okoye rolled her eyes.

Black Panther sped up to one of the SUVs as the vehicles made their way through the hilly streets of the Haeundae district. The driver of the SUV leaned out and opened fire on the rapidly approaching Black Panther car.

"Your suit, big bro. I'm getting high kinetic readings as the bullets hit you," Shuri noted from her lab, looking at her tablet.

"Just get me closer," Black Panther said in response.

"You could at least admit this suit's a lot better than your old helmet-head," Shuri muttered to herself as she remotely accelerated T'Challa's sports car.

The vehicle inched up until it was alongside the

SUV. When the driver was within arm's reach, Panther extended the claws built into his gloves and swiftly sliced the gun into pieces. He peered inside the car.

"No sign of Klaue," Black Panther said.

"Let's take a peek at fleeing car number three, then," Shuri said. Using her tablet, she pushed the sports car to its max speed and steered it toward the neighboring SUV speeding alongside. The car revved but came up just short of reaching the passenger side. "You're going as fast as I can get it," she informed her brother.

"Then I'll have to make a leap for it." Black Panther angled toward the SUV. His car was close enough to the other that he was certain he could make the jump. With a grunt, he launched himself into the air and landed on the side of the SUV. Black Panther scaled his way across the vehicle until he reached the passenger-side window and looked in. Klaue was not in this one, either.

"Rule this one out as well," Black Panther growled into his comm.

"Nakia, Okoye—that means you've got Klaue right in front of you," Shuri reported to the two women.

Nakia floored her car. "On it!"

Black Panther's suit glowed blue as he clung to the side of the SUV. The driver swerved to try to shake him, but he held fast. Looking behind him, he saw that the driver who had been shooting at him was speeding up, trying to ram into Black Panther's car. Recalling what Shuri had said about the kinetic buildup in his suit, T'Challa had an idea.

Black Panther leaped off the side of the SUV and back onto his car. "Bring me as close as possible," he instructed Shuri. The genius princess remotely piloted the car to within mere inches of the SUV Panther had just jumped from. "Hard right on my signal, sister," he told her.

"What signal?" Shuri asked, unsure of what her brother was planning. She didn't have to wait long for the answer.

Black Panther raised a fist and punched the side of the SUV. There was a loud *BANG* and a massive spark as the kinetic energy stored in his suit was transferred to the side of the SUV where he had struck it. As Black Panther's car peeled off to the right, T'Challa gave a slight smile. The SUV careened out of control and slammed into its companion's approaching vehicle.

"Two-for-one punch! *Now* what do you think of the suit?" Shuri asked, impressed.

"It is certainly battle-ready," Black Panther answered. "Now, take me to Klaue."

Shuri surveyed the virtual map on her table. "It looks like they are headed to the Gwangan Bridge. Yep, just turned onto Cheetah Street. Nakia and Okoye are closing in fast."

"Black Panther can't hog all the fun," Nakia's voice came through the comm as she inched closer to Klaue's SUV.

Inside his vehicle, Klaue smiled. Turning to his driver, he said, "Time to lose our pestering Wakandan friends, don't you think?" With that, he leaned out the passenger side.

Okoye pointed. "Eyes on Klaue." She noticed the foe begin to raise his prosthetic hand. "Nakia!" Okoye shouted.

The Dora Milaje warrior's cry came too late, as Klaue unleashed a sonic blast from his hand that smashed into their car. The vibranium casing absorbed the blast, but the car began to shake. Piece by piece, it began to dismantle in the middle of the street. Okoye and Nakia quickly unbuckled their seat belts as each grabbed on to their own car door. The doors flew off the car, and the warrior women rode on the debris like surfboards until they came to a halt. Looking ahead, they saw that Klaue's SUV was long gone.

"You are on your own, my king," Okoye radioed in as Black Panther sped past them in pursuit of Klaue.

Shuri looked at her map on the table. A new image had just appeared near the Gwangan Bridge. "It looks like he's got aerial company. A helicopter just entered range. Ten to one says that's his escape route," Shuri informed her brother.

"There will be no escape," Black Panther vowed as his car gained momentum.

Nakia and Okoye dusted themselves off as traffic zoomed around their dismantled car in the middle of the road. Suddenly, a sedan stopped next to them, and the passenger-side window rolled down. Agent Everett Ross was behind the wheel.

"You ladies need a ride?" Ross asked, flashing a smile.

"We're teaming up now?" Nakia asked, climbing in.

Ross's face darkened. "I'm just afraid of what your king will do now that he's in the catsuit. We need Klaue alive."

"Shuri can guide us there," Okoye said.

"Who's that?" Ross was confused.

"*Ooh*, he's pretty cute," Shuri's bright voice piped over the comms. "Just tell the American to head for the bridge. I have my own car to drive."

Okoye looked at Ross and tapped her ear. "Oh, just a little bug in my ear," she said, smiling. "Head to the bridge."

Ross gave Okoye a puzzled look, but hit the gas and followed her directions to the Gwangan Bridge.

A mile ahead on Cheetah Street, Black Panther's car gained on Klaue's SUV. The bridge drew nearer every second. "I need to get closer," Black Panther called out.

"I'm trying my best. Jeez, everybody needs something," Shuri said, turning her attention back to her table to try to give the car a boost of speed.

Black Panther's car inched up closer and closer to Klaue's vehicle. He saw his enemy lean out the passenger window and extend his arm. This time, Black Panther was prepared.

"Punch it fast, Shuri!" From her lab, Shuri pushed a button, and the car hit maximum speed.

"Are you going to ram him?" she asked.

"No, but we're about to lose this ride," Black Panther answered.

The car was feet away from the SUV when Klaue fired his sonic disrupter beam. As the sports car exploded, Black Panther dove toward the SUV, landing near the bottom of it. Extending his claws, he grabbed the back tire and pulled it with a mighty *RIIIIIIIIP*. Then he rolled off the car onto the street.

The SUV fell backward and swerved uncontrollably. It hit the sidewalk and started to flip over and over, coming to a stop near an outdoor café.

Klaue pulled himself halfway out the window and fired again at Black Panther. With a mighty leap, Panther dodged the blast, taking off at a run to reach the SUV before Klaue could escape.

Overhead, a helicopter hovered, Limbani piloting.

"Should I fire?" Limbani radioed.

Klaue chuckled. "Nah. I'll take care of this." He raised his prosthetic hand again toward Black Panther. "Here, kitty, kitty." The sonic blaster began to whirl as it recharged and powered up, readying another blast.

Black Panther launched himself directly at the SUV, reaching for Klaue. Just before the thief could fire, Black Panther grasped the prosthetic and tore it off. With his other hand, he pulled Klaue out of the SUV and threw him onto the ground.

"Too long have your crimes gone unanswered for. My father hunted you for decades; now I shall finish what he started," Black Panther snarled as he crouched above Klaue.

Just then, behind Black Panther and Klaue, a familiar-looking sedan skidded to a halt. Nakia jumped out of the car. "Stop!" she cried out.

Black Panther hesitated at the sound of his longtime friend's voice.

"Think! Is this what your father would want? You said Klaue must face his crimes. He can't do that if he's dead," Nakia continued as she approached Black Panther and Klaue.

Black Panther looked down at Klaue. He despised the man, reviled him; but Nakia was right. If he gave in to his impulses now, Klaue would never truly be brought to heel for all the pain and suffering he'd caused. "Blood for blood should not be our way," he said aloud to himself.

"What I thought. You don't have the stomach for it." Klaue laughed at Black Panther.

With a single fluid gesture, Black Panther sheathed his claws and formed a fist. "For my father!" he cried as he swung down and knocked out his nemesis with a single blow. Above, Limbani angled the helicopter away from the scene and flew out into the Haeundae harbor, making his escape, seeing the fight was lost—for now.

Black Panther hoisted the unconscious Klaue up over his shoulder and walked toward Nakia, Okoye, and Ross. Nakia smiled, and Okoye lowered her head in a slight bow to her king.

"You may interrogate him, but I wish to be present. After, he comes with us back to Wakanda," Panther said to Agent Ross. "And we keep the vibranium." He pulled the brown paper bag out of Klaue's jacket.

Ross chuckled. "Details to be worked out. Important thing is you got our man."

T'Challa gave a slight smile in return and thought of his father, how long Klaue had evaded T'Chaka. "Yes. I got him." *For you, Baba*, he thought.

As T'Challa loaded Klaue's limp frame into the waiting sedan, he caught sight of Nakia, still smiling proudly. He suddenly realized this was more than just tracking down a foe and capturing him. T'Challa had made a promise to the tribal elders, his first as the new king, to capture Klaue, and now he was successfully delivering on that promise. He looked to the sky and imagined his father's spirit looking down, smiling as well. For the first time since being declared king of Wakanda in the Challenge Pool, T'Challa finally felt confident he could lead. T'Challa finally felt worthy of the title of king.

BLACK PANTHER: AFTERMATH

BY STEVE BEHLING

Vengeance.

Vengeance for his father.

That's what was on Black Panther's mind as the snow crunched beneath his boots. He removed the fearsome helmet he wore as part of his uniform, set it on the ground, and drew in a deep breath of crisp, cold Siberian air. In front of him, sitting on a rocky cliff, was a quiet, unassuming man. The man didn't move. He didn't seem to notice the cold, and he didn't seem to notice Black Panther.

Every instinct T'Challa possessed screamed at him to despise this man. And yet, for a reason he couldn't begin to fathom, he could not bring himself to feel hatred.

"I almost killed the wrong man," T'Challa said, his voice slow and steady.

"The wrong man" had been Bucky Barnes, aka the Winter Soldier. Decades ago, Barnes had been fighting the good fight against the forces of Hydra in World War II. He fought valiantly against the enemy, alongside Captain America—his best friend, Steve Rogers. He was presumed dead during the last days of that war. It was only recently that Rogers learned otherwise—that Barnes had, in fact, lived but had been brainwashed somehow, turned into a lethal assassin.

T'Challa had believed that Barnes was responsible for the death of his father, T'Chaka.

But he now knew otherwise.

The man responsible sat on the cliff, looking into the open air before him. He didn't flinch at the sound of T'Challa's voice. It was as though he had been expecting him.

"Hardly an innocent one," the man said. He didn't turn around to address T'Challa. Instead, he just sat there, staring into the open expanse.

As he listened to the man's voice, T'Challa thought of his father. He was a good man—the king of Wakanda, an almost completely hidden African nation that had been taking its first tentative steps on the world stage when the United Nations had come together to sign the Sokovia Accords. The Accords would establish international controls over the Avengers, deciding where and when they would intervene. The principle was simple: to prevent a tragedy like Sokovia from happening again.

"Is it all you wanted?" T'Challa asked as he continued to walk toward the man on the cliff. "To see them rip each other apart?"

"Them" referred to the Avengers. Specifically, Captain America and Iron Man. Steve Rogers and Tony Stark.

The man on the cliff was Helmut Zemo. He had manipulated the Avengers into fighting against one another, pitting friend against friend, ally against ally. It was he who had led the Winter Soldier, Captain America, and Iron Man to this remote Siberian location. He who had orchestrated a bitter fight between the heroes. He who had hoped that they would destroy one another.

But why? For what? T'Challa fought back his own surprise when he discovered he needed answers to those questions.

T'Challa had traveled with his father to Vienna, where the summit had taken place. It was there that Zemo had set in motion his plan to pit Avenger against Avenger. There that Zemo's plan of retribution and revenge would take root. He'd bombed the meeting and made it appear as though Barnes had been the terrorist behind it.

The bombing had its casualties, of course.

Casualties like T'Challa's father, King T'Chaka.

That was why T'Challa had followed Cap to a remote location in Siberia.

Vengeance.

To confront Zemo. To exact revenge in the name of his father.

"My father lived outside the city," Zemo said slowly. He didn't look up as T'Challa drew closer to him. "I thought we would be safe there."

"There" was in Sokovia, or rather, right outside the capital city of that country. The place that became ground zero when the Avengers fought a last-ditch battle against Ultron, the artificial intelligence created by Tony Stark and Bruce Banner that had gone awry and decided the only way to protect humanity was to destroy it completely.

Ultron tried to use vibranium stolen from T'Challa's native country of Wakanda to raise a part of the capital city into the sky and bring it crashing down upon the earth—causing an extinction-level event.

The Avengers fought to save the citizens of Sokovia and, indeed, the world. As the landmass came falling toward the earth, Stark and the Asgardian Thor used their might to shatter it to pieces. The world was spared Ultron's intended fate, but it came with a terrible cost.

Human lives.

For though they had saved the world, the Avengers had been unable to save everyone in Sokovia. It seemed that someone—or someones—close to Zemo had been among those lost.

"My son was excited," Zemo said, a faint smile crossing his face. "He could see the Iron Man from the car window." In his right hand, Zemo held a loaded pistol.

He shook his head. "I told my wife, 'Don't worry. They're fighting in the city. We're miles from harm.'"

T'Challa stood next to Zemo now, hanging on his every word. A part of him said, *Take your vengeance. He is yours.* But Zemo's voice somehow spoke louder to him.

"When the dust cleared," Zemo said, his tone soft, "and the screaming stopped, it took me two days until I found their bodies. My father . . . still holding my wife and son in his arms."

Zemo shook his head again, his voice choked with emotion. "And the Avengers? They went home."

T'Challa looked at Zemo with a mixture of hatred and...something else. He couldn't quite put his finger on what he felt toward this man who had killed his father. All he knew was that the voice that called for vengeance was growing softer still.

"I knew I couldn't kill them," Zemo continued, his voice becoming stronger, more strident. "More powerful men than me have tried. But...if I could get them to kill each other..." His voice trailed off.

And there it was.

Vengeance.

The whole motivation behind Zemo's plan. He blamed the Avengers for the deaths of his beloved family. His revenge? To have the Avengers destroy one another, and barring that, themselves.

T'Challa moved in closer, his eyes fixed on the man he had pursued from Vienna to Siberia and on the weapon Zemo clutched tightly in his hand.

"I'm sorry about your father," Zemo said. His voice sounded sincere. Remorseful, even. "He seemed a good man."

For the first time, the sad man with the pistol in his right hand looked over his shoulder at T'Challa, and then returned his gaze to overlooking the cliff. "With a dutiful son."

T'Challa had been consumed by the need for revenge. It gnawed at him. But now, in the present, looking at Zemo, listening to his story, T'Challa could finally identify the emotion coursing through him.

It was pity.

"Vengeance has consumed you," T'Challa spoke quietly. "It's consuming them," he said, referring to Cap and Iron Man. "I'm done letting it consume me."

Zemo stared over the cliff. If he had heard T'Challa, he made no sign of it.

"Justice will come soon enough," T'Challa said.

Zemo's response was a bitter laugh. "Tell that to the dead," he said. He raised the gun as though to aim it toward himself.

But T'Challa reached out and stilled Zemo's hand, hauling him up from where he teetered on the cliff. "The living are not done with you yet," he said.

T'Challa realized he might as well have been speaking to himself.

CHAPTER 1

LATER THAT DAY. MUCH LATER.

The flight back from Siberia aboard the Royal Talon Fighter had been dull, uneventful, and exhausting. The air inside the cockpit was dry, and T'Challa's throat hurt. He was tired. His bones ached, his head throbbed, and his muscles were weary. So much had happened over the course of the last few days.

T'Challa realized that he hadn't eaten since his father's death. Nor had he slept. Even on this flight to Berlin, to remand Zemo into custody, he hadn't so much as closed his eyes.

If he was being honest with himself, T'Challa would have admitted that a part of him was afraid to sleep. Not because he thought that sleep would elude him, or that he would have nightmares.

T'Challa was afraid that, if he closed his eyes, he would see his father.

His Baba, his closest friend and greatest strength, whom he had failed to keep safe.

How could he face him? What would his father say? And what would he say to his father? How would T'Challa explain that he had been unable to prevent his death?

Then his thoughts drifted to his country. What would his father's death mean for Wakanda, for the people who had followed his father through fire and worse, to those who had believed in him?

What would it mean for T'Challa?

His heart ached with such loss as he had never experienced before, a void that could not be filled.

T'Challa felt utterly alone. Lost.

"What will become of him?" T'Challa asked, once he and Zemo had been escorted inside the Joint Terrorism Task Force government building. It was a black site in the city of Berlin, Germany—officially, it didn't exist.

He inclined his head slightly toward the cell containing Helmut Zemo. The glass was a two-way mirror—Zemo could not see out of the room, but T'Challa could see in. Zemo wore the same sadly vacant expression on his face that he had back in Siberia.

In fact, for all Zemo had spoken in Siberia, he'd spent the flight to Berlin in complete silence. To be fair, T'Challa hadn't engaged the man in conversation. Though he may have pitied Zemo, he could not bring himself to feel anything further for the man who had caused the death of his beloved father.

"What becomes of anybody?" was the reply that greeted T'Challa's ears. The voice belonged to Agent Everett Ross, who worked for the Joint Terrorism Task Force, a multinational agency. A dapper man with perfectly kept hair, Ross wore a sharp suit and had a razor-edged attitude to match. The two men had met only recently as a result of Zemo's plot, but T'Challa felt he had known the agent for far longer.

Misery acquaints a man with strange bedfellows, thought T'Challa.

T'Challa looked at Ross. He could have arched an eyebrow, but he didn't need to. His silence and the stony look on his face told Ross what the son of the Wakandan king really meant by his question.

"He'll be processed, we'll see what he'll tell us, if anything," Ross said, shrugging. "Does Zemo have anything else planned? Any 'Easter eggs' that he's hidden, surprises that we need to be worrying about? If he does, we'll find them. Then we'll take him to the Raft, where he'll enjoy the hospitality of our agency until he grows old and dies."

T'Challa nodded. He knew the Raft was an underwater prison, its precise location unknown. If a person was unfortunate or evil enough to earn a trip there, odds were the ticket was one-way. He looked over Ross's shoulders, into the cell behind him. Zemo stared into nothingness. The man sat calmly, breathing in, breathing out. He looked harmless. It was hard to believe this man very nearly, single-handedly, took down the Avengers.

And yet.

"I'm sure he thinks his plan worked," Ross said. "Can you imagine?"

"In his own way, he's a victim," T'Challa said softly. "How many more in Sokovia are like him? The tragedy that befell Zemo...it could consume anyone."

Ross picked up a folder from a desk and shoved it under his arm. "Yeah, well, most people who experience tragedy don't try to get Iron Man to destroy Captain America."

The man has a point, T'Challa thought.

"Now, is there anything else you can do for us?" Ross asked as he sat down behind a desk. T'Challa stood, looking at the odd man.

"I...I do not understand," T'Challa responded, shaking his head. "I have delivered Zemo to you. I should think any obligation, if one existed, has been met."

"Obligation? Who's talking about obligations? I'm talking about...a limited partnership," Ross replied.

"A limited partnership," T'Challa said, drawing out the words. "Speak plainly, Agent Ross. My country has urgent need of me."

"Please. 'Agent Ross' sounds so formal, I feel like I'm in trouble," the agent said with a smile. "Call me Everett."

"Agent Ross," T'Challa repeated. He did not smile back. "Please, come to the point."

Ross leaned back in his office chair and put his feet up on his desk, resisting the urge to roll his eyes. He drew his hands behind his head, locking the fingers together to make a headrest. Then he smiled.

What kind of a man is this Agent Ross? T'Challa wondered.

"Before he started this little party," Ross began, "Zemo had been staying at a boardinghouse nearby. What if I told you we found something in the room Zemo was renting? Something that might cause a whole lot of problems for a whole lot of innocent people?"

T'Challa leaned forward intently and crossed his arms. Wakanda beckoned him home, but a part of him was terrified of returning to his native land to face a people racked by sadness and an uncertain future, all because of him. If he could prolong his stay overseas by just a little bit and do something good, maybe he could find a bit of peace.

"Okay, Agent Ross. I am listening."

CHAPTER 2

BERLIN, GERMANY. TWENTY MINUTES LATER.

Everett Ross was not a happy-go-lucky man. While he wore the facade of a glib person, always quick with a quip or a joke, Ross had to admit that, underneath, he was perpetually anxious and concerned: about the state of his agency, the safety of his agents, and the myriad threats to the security of the United States—and the world—that they faced off against every day. He fought hard not to show it, but sometimes it came out.

"My apologies, Your Highness," Ross said to T'Challa after he'd met up with the Wakandan prince and after his interrogation of Zemo. "I'm a little on edge. Please, bear with me."

Together, they walked down a plain, unmarked hallway.

"We went over the room Zemo was renting with a fine-tooth comb," Ross said. "I don't even know what that is, *a fine-tooth comb*, but I was assured the team used one. Went over everything."

The duo stopped at a plain doorway marked with a simple red bar on the door. Ross walked up to the bar. A glowing line moved from the top of the bar to the bottom, panning Ross's face.

"Retina scan," Ross explained, a hint of pride in his voice.

The bar then changed from red to green, and the door swung open. Ross turned around to T'Challa with a look that said, *Impressive, huh?*

T'Challa did not look impressed. The technology in Wakanda far surpassed the technology of the outside world, on all levels. A door that changed colors and opened itself wasn't going to move the needle with T'Challa.

Ross shrugged at T'Challa's impassive response, and then motioned for him to step inside and followed behind him.

Jeez, thought Ross. *This guy has absolutely no sense of humor.*

Once inside the conference room, T'Challa saw a large

monitor at one end. On the screen was a static image of Zemo, a file photo. Next to Zemo's image was a photograph of the boardinghouse where he had been staying shortly before he set his plan in motion.

"Let's get down to business," Ross began, gesturing for T'Challa to sit. "Zemo. For such a secretive guy, he really liked to write things down. I mean, a lot. He left a handwritten journal behind at the boardinghouse." Ross waved his hand in front of the monitor, and the image changed, displaying a photograph of a leather-bound book sealed in a plastic evidence bag.

T'Challa was still standing, listening to Ross, staring at the monitor. He hadn't said a word.

"You sure you don't want to sit down?" Ross asked. "You look uncomfortable. It's making *me* uncomfortable. I hate feeling uncomfortable. Please, have a seat."

T'Challa slowly took a seat next to Ross. His eyes never left the monitor.

So serious, Ross thought with a mental roll of his eyes.

"Okay, so, the journal. Zemo filled the whole book using a code. Given the time, I have no doubt our cryptographers would have been able to crack the code and translate the entire book. Then we would have known the full scope of Zemo's plans and could have prevented anything else he had in mind."

T'Challa cocked his head. "What do you mean, 'would have been able to crack'? Where is the journal now?"

Ross clapped his hands together. "Perfect. I knew you'd pick up on it. See, *this* is why I wanted us to work together." Ross smiled at T'Challa, who did not return the grin.

Sheesh, Ross thought. *So much for the charm offensive.*

Ross pushed on. "I used past tense to indicate that we don't currently have the journal in our possession," he said. He waved his hand in front of the monitor once more. The image of the journal was replaced with a photograph of an unremarkable-looking woman. She appeared to be in her midforties, with straight black hair. She had a mole on her right cheek and a pair of rectangular glasses perched on her nose. "She has it."

"Who is she?" T'Challa asked.

Ross clapped his hands again. "We are gonna get along fine, you and me," Ross said. "She was a trusted member of our organization, or so we thought. Her name is

Charmagne Sund. At least, that's the name she gave us. Could be real, could be an alias, who knows."

"I don't understand," T'Challa said, looking at the image on the screen more closely. "How does someone become a member of your organization, and then—"

"Betray said organization by stealing vital evidence from an ongoing investigation?" Ross added quickly, finishing T'Challa's sentence. "Excellent question. We're trying to figure that out. But more important is that she has the book, and she's gone."

"When?"

"Half hour ago, give or take a few minutes," Ross said. "Near as we can figure, while I was in there talking with Zemo, Sund was in the evidence room, taking the journal. Security cameras recorded her entering the room, then leaving our facility immediately thereafter."

"Why would she want the journal?" T'Challa asked.

"I was kind of hoping you could find her and ask that very question," Ross said. He waved his hand over the monitor, and the screen went black.

CHAPTER 3

Though he was standing in the conference room with Everett Ross, T'Challa found his thoughts drifting to the weighty matters that had occupied his every waking moment of late.

Fate.

Vengeance.

The lives of two men, so different, yet intertwined.

T'Challa was torn between his heart and his head. In his heart, he knew that he must return home to Wakanda. With his father dead, the tribes needed him. His people needed him. His family...his sister needed him. His mother needed him.

His mother. Ramonda, the Queen Mother.

How could he look her in the eyes after what happened?

How could he tell her that one moment, he had been talking to her beloved husband, and the next, saying good-bye?

For the first time since the bomb had gone off at the United Nations summit, T'Challa found himself fighting back tears.

Overcome with emotion, T'Challa thought more about what his father's death meant to Wakanda. Arrangements had to be made. As next in line to become king, T'Challa would take part in a ceremony at Warrior Falls. It was an ancient ritual, and rituals were incredibly important to the people of Wakanda. This ritual required the presence of the four tribes: the Border Tribe, the Mining Tribe, the Merchant Tribe, and the River Tribe. One challenger from each tribe could contest T'Challa's right to the throne, and he would have to fight each in turn and emerge victorious; alternatively, they could cede the throne to him, and he would automatically be made king.

Either way, by battle or by birthright, it seemed the kingship would be his.

But did he want it?

His heart was firmly planted in Wakanda. It belonged to his father, his family, his people.

But his head was another thing entirely.

T'Challa had seen firsthand what kind of destruction Zemo was capable of committing. He had experienced the chaos caused by a man who had allowed vengeance to take root in his soul and grow unchecked. Zemo's thirst for vengeance had killed T'Challa's father. It had killed innocent people.

What if that man had more chaos to unleash on the world? What if this Charmagne Sund were to somehow use the knowledge from Zemo's journal to sow such chaos? What if she turned that journal, that knowledge, over to someone with even more sinister intentions? As he had seen, the world was full of such menaces. From Ultron to Baron Strucker, from Klaue to Zemo, there was no shortage of evil.

Torn between his duty to Wakanda and his sense of responsibility to the larger world around him, T'Challa found himself at a crossroads. What would his father say to him if he were here at this moment? he wondered. T'Challa's mind began to drift back to the last conversation between father and son.

At the United Nations, in Vienna.

Before the bomb.

"For a man who disapproves of diplomacy," T'Chaka said to T'Challa in their native Wakandan tongue, "you're getting quite good at it." The older man placed his right hand on his son and smiled warmly.

It was true. T'Challa wasn't sure about this move, of opening the doors of Wakanda to the world at large. But he trusted his father more than anything. And if it was something his father believed to be so important, then T'Challa would fight for it.

T'Challa grinned back. "I'm happy, Father," he said. "I believe in what we're doing here. I believe in you."

"Thank you," T'Chaka said. He had wanted Wakanda to step out from behind its veil of secrecy. He believed the world at large had need of Wakanda, and Wakanda of the world around them. T'Chaka would lead them, but he needed his son, T'Challa, to accompany him on the journey.

Those were the last words T'Challa and his father exchanged.

"Prince T'Challa? Are you with me?" Ross said, waving a hand in front of T'Challa's face. "I asked if you would help us."

T'Challa snapped back to the present and looked Ross in the eyes. "My father would have wanted me to help you," T'Challa said in response. "But why me? You have all the agents you could possibly need."

"You're right, I have more agents than I can count. That's not true, actually; I have eighty-four. But none of them are you. None of them are Black Panther," Ross said. "And something tells me I'm gonna need Black Panther for this one."

The words lingered in T'Challa's ears for a moment before he said, "Very well. But I have a duty to my people as well."

Ross nodded. "Of course, of course. Believe me, this will be quick. All we need you to do is to track down Sund and deliver the journal back to us."

"Do we know where she was likely to go?" T'Challa asked.

Ross splayed out his hands. "Yes and no? She's still in

Berlin. No sign of her at the borders or airports," he said. "I have a lead that we can follow. That, and I'm going to guess you're pretty good at tracking things."

T'Challa nodded.

"I am the Black Panther, after all," he said.

"Of course you are," Ross said. "Come on, Black Panther, let's take a ride."

I like driving in Berlin," Ross said from behind the wheel of a nondescript black sedan. "They drive on the right. It's just like back home."

T'Challa sat in the passenger seat, his Black Panther helmet pulled down over his face. He listened to the sound of traffic coming from outside the sedan. The sun made its presence known through the tinted windows, and T'Challa could tell it was late afternoon.

Ross looked at his companion, and then returned his eyes to the road. *What a pair we make*, he thought.

"Take England," Ross said as they made their way through the heavy traffic on Unter den Linden. The street cut through the central Mitte district of Berlin and was always busy. Ross honked his horn, and T'Challa noticed that no other drivers were honking theirs. "They drive on the left in England. I get turned around. Every time I drive in England, I get into an accident. I just can't wrap my brain around it. You're lucky you're on a mission with me in Berlin."

T'Challa turned and looked out the window, and Ross could tell he was losing him. "What is this 'lead' you have?" asked the prince of Wakanda. "Why are we in this car?"

Ross tilted his head as he looked at the road in front of him. "I'm gonna fill you in on a little secret. All employees of the agency are implanted with microchips so we can track them, should they become lost, get kidnapped—"

"Or betray the agency," T'Challa cut in.

"Exactly. The great thing about these microchips is, none of the people in the agency know they have them."

"Then how do you know about them?" T'Challa asked.

"That," Ross shot back, "is a really good question. One of the best. And the answer is, because it's on a need-to-know basis, and I need to know."

T'Challa shot Ross a look that said, *How can I trust a man like you?*

Or maybe I'm just reading too much into it, Ross thought.

"I know it sounds bad, but trust me, we do this kind of thing for a reason."

"I do not know what to think of you or an agency where privacy can be so easily discarded," T'Challa said, looking back out the passenger window. "Where is Charmagne Sund now?"

Ross glanced down at his phone. "According to her microchip, she's up there," Ross said, pointing through the windshield. He gestured at a large building with a stone facade.

Before Ross could say another word, T'Challa spoke. "That is the Berlin State Opera," he said.

"See?" Ross said, a jaunty tone in his voice. "You work with me, you also get some culture."

T'Challa very nearly cracked a smile just as a hail of bullets shattered the windshield.

It happened so fast, Ross could hardly keep track of it all.

First, it was the bullets. They hammered the windshield, causing the safety glass to crack like a spiderweb. The bullets sliced through the vehicle's armor plating as if it weren't even there. The armor should have stopped anything short of a tank shell, but Ross didn't have time to unpack the questions racing through his head.

Then the tires. The sound of all four tires blowing out filled Ross's ears. At once, he lost control of the speeding vehicle. The car skidded on the street, slammed into another car, and flipped over.

Finally, the car. Ross and T'Challa found themselves upside down as the sedan, now turned onto its roof, spun around in a circle as bullets continued to rain down. T'Challa unbuckled himself and, in a flash, unbuckled Ross as well. He grabbed the agent, and then kicked out the driver's-side door. He shielded Ross with his body, rolling both of them out of harm's way.

Or very nearly.

T'Challa winced as he felt a bullet graze his left arm, a blinding flash of red-hot, searing pain coursing through his body. The vibranium bodysuit he wore should have deadened the impact of any normal bullet. This bullet was something else altogether.

Crouched behind the still-spinning car, Ross caught his bearings. "The bullets are coming from a window. Top floor, State Opera," he called out.

"Stay down," T'Challa instructed as he tenderly pressed his left arm, assessing the damage.

Blood.

"Take this!" Ross shouted, and threw a small tube-shaped device to T'Challa. "Comm link!"

Without saying another word or pausing to think about his bleeding arm, T'Challa was gone. He leaped over the wrecked car and darted across the street toward the State Opera. His legs pumped, faster and faster, as he built up speed. Then, with an incredible leap that defied belief, the Black Panther threw himself into the air, clung to the side of the stone building, and began to claw his way upward.

CHAPTER 5

T'Challa wanted to believe that his father was right. That Wakanda should assume its rightful place in the world and join the international community. T'Chaka felt strongly about that. He felt so strongly, in fact, that he died for his beliefs.

T'Challa wanted to believe that his father was right, but he wasn't sure.

He hated himself for that.

All this and more raced through T'Challa's mind as he scurried up the stone facade of the Berlin State Opera. Razor-sharp claws forged from vibranium dug into the stonework, while muscles honed through years of intense training did the rest. It appeared effortless.

Black Panther reached the top floor in seconds and was at the window from which the shots were fired. In a fluid motion, he dragged the claws of his right hand across the glass of a closed window, and then pushed inward. The glass fell in, and T'Challa flung himself through the now-open window. He tucked into a roll, and as he came out of it, he stuck his feet to the ground and stopped in a crouched position.

No one was there.

T'Challa threw open a door and looked down a long hallway. To his left, to his right, there was no one. Nothing seemed amiss.

Except for a handful of fragments and shards of some sort scattered on the floor. T'Challa bent to pick one of them up. What he had thought were bullets raining down on them were, in fact, not bullets at all. But before he had time to examine it closer, a voice crackled over the comm link that Ross had given him.

"Talk to me, what do we have?"

Agent Ross.

T'Challa drew a deep breath, and then exhaled. "We have a ghost. There is no one here," he said, staring at the fragment in the palm of his left hand. "The shooter is gone. Where, I cannot tell."

"You can tell me, I'm a fully deputized agent," Ross said, trying to inject a little levity into the situation.

T'Challa didn't laugh.

"Sorry," Ross replied. "I've lost track of Sund. Something's interfering with the microchip. My team will canvass the area. Looks like we're back to square one."

"I said the *shooter* is gone. But she has left something behind." T'Challa took another good, hard look at the fragment he held in his hand. Something about it looked familiar. Then he recognized what it was and could scarcely believe it.

It was made of vibranium.

T'Challa felt the throbbing in his left arm.

"You know, I have to admit, I'm disappointed. I was looking forward to a front-seat view of you engaged in some kind of daring chase with the shooter," Ross said.

"Life is not all about the chase," T'Challa said gravely, as he walked with Ross to a fresh black sedan that had seemingly appeared out of nowhere. "That is something my father understood."

The local police had secured the area, and Ross's team was sweeping the immediate vicinity of the State Opera, looking for additional clues.

"I understand that, too, believe me," Ross replied as he opened the driver's door to the new sedan. T'Challa got in and shut the door quickly.

"These fragments the shooter was using are made of vibranium," Black Panther said bluntly.

"That's how they pierced the armored car and your suit so easily," Ross mused. T'Challa nodded. "Where did Charmagne Sund get vibranium?"

"There is only one source of vibranium in the world," T'Challa said slowly. "Wakanda. And you know we did not provide it. There is only one man I know of who has dealt in vibranium."

"Klaue?" Ross asked. He meant Ulysses Klaue, a disreputable, dishonest, often murderous arms dealer who had, among other things, stolen a cache of vibranium from Wakanda some time ago. The theft incurred the wrath of T'Challa's father, and all of Wakanda. Klaue's crimes against humanity were quite literally too numerous to mention. "Do you think Klaue's behind this?"

T'Challa considered Ross's question as the car started up and pulled away. "I do not. But I think some of the vibranium he stole has ended up with Charmagne Sund.

The question is, who gave it to her? Find the answer to that and perhaps we will know to whom she plans on delivering the journal."

"Your grammar is terrific," Ross said, shaking his head as they swung a sharp left around a corner. "Mine, not so much. But yours? I wish I had your gift."

To his own surprise, the thinnest of smiles crept upon T'Challa's face.

"You are an interesting man, Agent Ross."

CHAPTER 6

Just drive.

Her breath was heavy, but measured. She had lost all track of time from the moment she'd grabbed the journal. Her mind raced as she did her best to get her bearings and keep calm.

A moment ago, Charmagne Sund had been at a window in the top floor of the State Opera, firing off rounds at the unmarked black sedan. She recognized the make and model immediately and knew it belonged to the agency. She had expected it, even counted on it.

After all, that was part of her plan.

What she hadn't expected was a man with sharp claws and a skintight black costume to come bounding up the wall of the State Opera. She knew who it was. She had read Ross's file on the man.

T'Challa, prince of Wakanda. The Black Panther.

She clutched the leather-bound book tightly in her left hand, and the steering wheel in the other. Sund had moved quickly the moment she saw Black Panther. Descending into the opera house itself, she made her way through the grand, ornate interiors to the street below, and then out a side door. From there, it was a simple matter to procure a parked car, hot-wire it, and drive away unnoticed.

For now, at least. At this point, Ross would have half the agency combing the streets of Berlin looking for her. No way could she leave the city undetected.

That was fine, because Sund had no intention of leaving Berlin. But she did have somewhere else she needed to be.

Sund wondered if she should have ever taken the journal in the first place. The agency would almost surely see it as an act of betrayal and send out assassination teams to terminate her. At least, that's what she believed they would do.

Why *had* she taken the book? She didn't even want it.

She was almost afraid of it, of the information it contained. Helmut Zemo was a bitter, twisted man who sought to bring down a team of heroes for...what? Justice? Vengeance? His family was dead. Zemo's actions wouldn't help them.

And yet, justice and vengeance were two emotions Sund could identify with strongly.

Very strongly.

So she knew that a person who would go to those ends for revenge could be capable of almost anything. Whatever else was in the journal, whatever plans Zemo may have had—may still have—would be inside. Though the pages were coded, Sund knew that any cryptographer worth their salt could decode it. And once they did, that information would be valuable currency throughout the criminal underworld.

People would come looking for it.

Zemo himself would come looking for it.

That's right, Sund thought to herself. *Zemo will come.* Did Ross really think the agency could hold Zemo? He had already masterminded a mind-bogglingly complex scheme involving an electromagnetic pulse that depowered the agency's headquarters in Berlin, shutting down all power, allowing the Winter Soldier to escape.

That was how Zemo's plan to destroy the Avengers had reached its next level.

Could anyone truly believe that Zemo was no longer a threat?

Sund didn't think so. And she meant to neutralize the threat before it could do any more damage. After all, it was what she'd been trained to do. She owed it to the world.

Most important, she owed it to the people of Sokovia— a country she loved, a country whose name would be forever linked with Zemo.

Unless she did something about it.

As she sped down Unter den Linden, away from the State Opera, she listened to the sirens wailing in the distance.

Vengeance.

CHAPTER 7

The agency was mostly empty. Most of the personnel had been called to the State Opera and were conducting the investigation under Ross's orders. Ross himself had returned to headquarters with T'Challa, trying to make sense of everything that had happened.

T'Challa stood in front of Ross's desk, his black-gloved fingers sifting through an unmarked file folder that was spread out before him. There was a file photo of Charmagne Sund, along with her biographical information. T'Challa held the vibranium fragment in his left hand, rolling it around his palm as he read the file.

Ross split his attention between T'Challa, the Sund file, and the phone glued to his ear. He was in the middle of a conversation that appeared particularly one-sided, evidenced by the way he held the receiver a good six inches from his ear.

"Yes, sir, I—" was all Ross managed to spit out before the shouting on the other end of the phone commenced again. "Yes, sir, I know, you need to be involved in anything relating to the Avengers, but—" The angry voice picked up steam. All Ross could do was roll his eyes and wait for the tirade to finish.

T'Challa looked up at Ross as the agent covered the mouthpiece of his phone.

"Believe it or not, this is pretty standard," Ross said, grinning. "Always a pleasure to receive a dressing-down from the secretary of state."

The secretary of state was a different Ross: Thaddeus Ross—or "Thunderbolt" Ross, as he was known in his army days. He had spent years spearheading a top-secret project that sought to re-create the Super-Soldier experiment that transformed frail Steve Rogers into the incredible physical specimen known as Captain America. Except Ross's experiments ended a little differently, resulting in a scientist named Bruce Banner becoming the rampaging Hulk, and Ross's own man, Emil Blonsky, transforming into the Abomination.

T'Challa suppressed a chuckle. "Why does the secretary of state waste his time calling you, when you have an investigation to run?"

"Exactly," Ross shot back, hand still over the receiver while the screaming continued over the phone. "Ever since Sokovia and the Accords, Ross wants to be looped into anything remotely involving the Avengers. In this case, it means you, and the shooting at the opera house."

"I am not an Avenger," T'Challa contested flatly.

"Try telling that to 'Thunderbolt' Ross. To him, anyone wearing fancy pajamas is an Avenger." Ross sighed heavily, and then sat in his chair. "We're not related, you know. In case you were wondering."

"Really? I am surprised. In Wakanda, we assume that everyone with the last name *Ross* must be related," T'Challa said. His eyes never left the file in front of him.

Ross looked at T'Challa, and then pointed at him, accidentally uncovering the receiver. He started to shake his finger. "Wait, was that—did you just make a joke?" he asked excitedly. "Did the prince of Wakanda just make a joke? I think that was a joke."

Violent screaming erupted from the phone, causing Ross to grimace.

I forgot about the darn phone, Ross thought.

"No, sir, I didn't think *you* were joking," Ross said into the phone, his tone placating. "Of course not. Nothing you say is a joke, and I take every word with incredible importance."

As T'Challa continued to scan the Sund file, something caught his eye.

"Sokovia," he said.

Ross tilted his head. "Sokovia?"

More screaming over the phone.

"No, sir, I don't want you to go to Sokovia. It's just, I really need to get back to this—"

T'Challa spoke over Ross. "Charmagne Sund is from Sokovia. That explains how she obtained the vibranium."

"How?" Ross asked, puzzled.

"Klaue turned a supply of vibranium over to Ultron to use in perfecting his robotic form. After the Battle of Sokovia, there would have been vibranium fragments left behind. She could have gathered the bits and pieces."

"And what, forged bullets?"

T'Challa shook his head. "That is doubtful. But she could be firing the shards and fragments, like shot in a shotgun. Just as deadly."

At that moment, a junior agent appeared at Ross's door, panting. "Sir, explosions all along Unter den Linden," she blurted out.

"You'll have to yell at me later, sir," Ross said into the phone, hitting the END button. He nailed the junior agent with a hard gaze. "Okay. Tell us everything you know."

The junior agent standing in Ross's doorway delivered an incredible amount of information in an equally incredibly short amount of time. Ross was flat-out impressed. Or he would have been impressed, if he wasn't so angry.

The explosions began around three o'clock that afternoon. They occurred all along the busy Unter den Linden, stretching from the Schlossbrücke at the east end to the Brandenburg Gate to the west.

In each instance, the blasts themselves caused little damage. Surprisingly, no civilians had been injured. But they drew the focus of the police as well as Ross's agency, when they were already stretched thin investigating the opera house shooting.

"What is going on here?" Ross asked out loud. He was met with silence. "No one answer—I wasn't really asking; that's just me thinking out loud."

The junior agent hovered in the doorway, not quite sure what she should do now that her presentation was complete. "Do you want me to stay or...?" she said, her voice trailing off.

"I want you to monitor this situation and report to me every five minutes," Ross said. "How long have you been with us?"

The junior agent shifted on her feet. "Three months, sir."

Ross nodded. "Three months. I can't believe it took you only three months to get promoted."

"But I—" the junior agent started to say, before realizing what Ross meant. She allowed herself a small smile, and then she nodded curtly and strode out of Ross's office.

"What is the connection between the shooting and the blasts, and the theft of the journal?" Ross wondered. "It's a whole bunch of seemingly unconnected stuff that is obviously connected, but it doesn't make any sense. None of it does."

T'Challa bit his lip, seeming just as flummoxed as Ross was by the random string of events. It was the first indication that Ross had yet seen that the prince of Wakanda was anything but entirely calm, cool, and collected twenty-four hours a day, seven days a week.

"Charmagne Sund is the connection," T'Challa suddenly announced.

Okay, maybe not.

"Charmagne Sund?" Ross asked. "I agree she was behind the shooting at the opera house. But the explosions, too? That seems a little too coincidental. Why would she do that? What's the point? Wouldn't she just escape with the journal?"

T'Challa stood up, shaking his head. "It is no coincidence. Charmagne Sund wants what Zemo wanted. What I, too, once wanted."

Ross sat behind his desk, raising his eyebrows, shaking his head as if to say, "And that is . . . ?"

"Vengeance."

And at that moment, for the second time in a week, the power went out, and Ross's office was plunged into darkness.

From the moment the power went out and the facility went dark, T'Challa understood what was happening. He could sense it. Perhaps it was instinct, based on all those years of training under his father. Learning the art of combat, tracking and hunting from warriors like the Dora Milaje—the special forces of Wakanda.

Or was it something else? Something deeper?

Maybe it was the strange kinship he had felt with Zemo. As much as T'Challa didn't like it, he had to admit the two men shared a terrible bond, one forged in grief.

Zemo had lost his family as the Avengers battled against Ultron in Sokovia. The loss he endured drove him to his incredible acts of vengeance.

T'Challa had lost his father to the bombing in Vienna, an unintended victim of Zemo's wrath.

Two men, consumed by vengeance.

One had succumbed to the urge and, in doing so, had lost his soul, his essence, his very being.

One had overcome it, managing to save himself in the process.

T'Challa felt a chill at the thought of another victim in all this, another person consumed by vengeance, driven to destroy. Could this dangerous cycle of vengeance be broken? he wondered.

T'Challa believed that it was Sund—knew it was her, in fact. It had to be. She was Sokovian. She was seeking vengeance of her own.

The journal had merely been a ruse—a red herring. It wasn't the endgame.

No, the endgame was vengeance.

And now T'Challa knew against whom. And he knew when and where.

It was here—inside the very headquarters of Ross's agency—and now.

"She is here," T'Challa said, his trained eyes rapidly adjusting to the darkness, pushing back from his chair and striding to the door of the office.

"What? Who?" Ross asked.

"Charmagne Sund," T'Challa said quietly. "We have to get to Zemo. Now."

"Why?"

"Because Sund is going to kill him."

Like everywhere else in the agency, it was dark in Helmut Zemo's holding cell. This genuinely surprised him. The last time he'd been inside the agency, he'd masqueraded as a psychiatrist to assess the Winter Soldier. When the power went out that time, it was a direct result of the electromagnetic bomb he set off.

This time it had nothing to do with him.

So if not him, then what? Or whom?

Zemo was resigned to the situation, sitting in his cell. He could do nothing. He wasn't super-powered, like the Winter Soldier, so there would be no breaking free of his holding cell. And even if he could break free and flee this place, what would be the point?

His family was still dead.

"It should have come back on by now," Ross panted as he and T'Challa raced through the darkened halls of the agency. "It came back on right after the pulse, last time."

"This is not last time," T'Challa said evenly. "You are dealing with someone who knows the inner workings of your system this time."

"I don't get it," Ross said. "Why would Sund do this? Why take the journal? Why lead us on a wild-goose chase? Why set off those bombs?"

"To distract you," T'Challa answered matter-of-factly. "To tie up your agents all over Berlin, have them chasing shadows . . . while she comes here, to a mostly empty building, to finish Zemo."

"'Finish'?" Ross exclaimed. "Hey, no one gets 'finished' on Joint Terrorism Task Force soil."

"Your agency might not do this," T'Challa said. "But a person from Sokovia with vengeance on her mind? She does."

The cell was quiet and still, and the air was stifling.

Zemo didn't care. Comfort was not exactly important to the man at the moment.

He sat on the hard-backed chair they'd provided for him, staring up at the ceiling, which he could not see because of the darkness. He thought it odd that no one had come to check on him, to make sure he wasn't trying to escape. Then again, it seemed especially strange to him that he should hear almost no commotion whatsoever.

What was Ross up to?

That's when the door to his cell opened. Zemo could hear someone breathing, but in the darkness, he could not see who it was.

"Helmut Zemo?" a voice rang out through the void. "Come with me."

Zemo didn't recognize the voice except that it was female. But he understood the tone.

It was the same tone that Zemo had in his voice when he spoke to Captain America and Iron Man in the cold silo in Siberia.

He had no choice. Zemo stood up and followed the voice through the inky blackness and out of his cell.

CHAPTER 11

Before Ross could say anything else, T'Challa raced down the hallway in pursuit. Thanks to the heart-shaped herb he ingested as Black Panther, he could see in the dark as if it were daytime—even better, in fact. His unimpaired vision and the unique properties of the vibranium woven into his suit rendered even his footsteps mute. Here, in the darkness, Black Panther maneuvered like his namesake: silent, stealthy, and ready to pounce.

Behind him, he could hear Ross calling through his comm for agents to return to the facility.

They won't get here in time to make a difference, T'Challa thought.

Less than a minute later, Black Panther arrived at Zemo's cell. He saw the door was open. Careful not to make a sound, he ducked his head into the cell.

Empty.

"They are gone," Black Panther said into the comm link. There was a brief hiss of static.

"Gone?" came a voice over the link. Ross. "What do you mean, 'gone'? Gone where?"

Black Panther looked around the cell and saw nothing amiss—not counting an absent Zemo as "amiss." He thought for a moment, trying to imagine what Sund would do, seeking vengeance.

He thought of Zemo and the cliff.

Then he had it.

"The roof," Black Panther said, and he was off.

There was a helipad atop the agency, but the altercation between the Winter Soldier and Captain America had damaged it. While it wasn't functional at the moment, the roof itself was still accessible through a rooftop entrance.

That was exactly where Zemo found himself at the moment—on the roof, and about to go over the edge and plummet to the ground far, far below.

A woman stood in front of him, the disembodied voice

from his cell come to life, her jet-black hair blowing in the wind as she trained her weapon directly at Zemo's heart. Zemo's leather-bound journal was clutched under her left arm.

If Zemo was concerned for his life, it wasn't readily apparent.

If he was afraid, he showed no sign of it.

"Am I to die?" Zemo asked without any trace of resistance. His voice was cool and emotionless. "Please, tell me why so I can thank you."

Charmagne Sund drew a slow breath, exhaled, and then renewed her grasp on the weapon in her hand. "I am from Sokovia, too," she said.

Zemo said nothing in reply. He didn't feel the need.

The Black Panther climbed up the side of the building using his suit's built-in vibranium claws. He'd thought about taking the stairs but had decided that bursting through the door on the roof not only eliminated any element of surprise but could also endanger Zemo's life.

Zemo's life.

It struck T'Challa as the height of irony that he of all people should be so concerned about the life of Helmut Zemo.

And yet it was so.

As he made his way up the wall, to the corner of the roof, Black Panther peered over. He saw Charmagne Sund, her back to him. She had a weapon pointed at Zemo, who teetered on the edge of the roof. It was clear to him what was about to happen.

"Bast, no," T'Challa whispered.

It was all happening so fast. Too fast.

Charmagne Sund, weapon in hand.

Zemo, on the edge of the roof.

Black Panther, creeping silently toward them, just out of sight.

"You and your plans," Sund spat at Zemo. "This book of yours." She shook the journal she still clutched in one hand. "You have ruined the name of Sokovia for all time. When people think of our country, now they will think of a madman. A maniac. A murderer."

Zemo stood in his spot on the roof and said nothing. What was there to say? Anything? Nothing he could say would change the past. It wouldn't bring the dead back to life.

"And don't tell me that killing you won't solve any-thing," she said, her voice tinged with barely concealed anger. "Because it will. When the world learns that Zemo is gone, then Sokovia's good name will be restored."

"Not this way."

Sund whirled around, startled to see Black Panther standing only five feet behind her.

She fired her weapon.

Black Panther leaned back, very nearly falling over, before catching himself. The fragments of vibranium exploded past him, but a small piece caught him on his right side, just below his ribs. It tore through his own vibranium suit as if it weren't there, leaving a bright red gash. He righted himself and held his left hand to his right side, squeezing tightly. Beneath his helmet, he grimaced.

Before he could make another move, Sund whipped back around and turned the gun on Zemo, striding over to him and grabbing him by his neck. She shoved the weapon into Zemo's chest.

"Not this way," Black Panther repeated, panting. With his right hand, he grabbed his helmet and removed it.

"You don't know what this monster has done," she shouted, her face a frozen mask of anger.

"I, of all people, know what he has done," said T'Challa

calmly. "That is why I, of all people, am telling you that you must let go of your need for vengeance."

"All those people!" she screamed, and grabbed Zemo's throat even harder. She threw an accusing look at Black Panther. "Your own father! How can you let him live?"

"His life is not yours or mine to take. We are not gods," Black Panther said, walking forward slowly. "We do not sit in judgment. Put your weapon away."

"Don't come any closer!" Sund shouted, and shoved the barrel into Zemo's chest so hard the man grunted in response.

"If you kill him, it will bring no honor to Sokovia," Black Panther reasoned. "Your country has suffered. Your people have suffered. What happened in Sokovia was a tragedy. But this man has suffered, too. He chose the path of vengeance. You are continuing his path. Do not."

Then a shot rang out in Black Panther's ears.

Everett Ross stood in the rooftop door, weapon in hand.

He had fired the shot. It found its mark in Charmagne Sund's right hand.

Sund stood near Zemo, cradling her wounded hand. There was blood. She had released her grip on Zemo. Zemo stood on the edge of the roof, unmoving, looking into the vast depths that spanned beyond the building.

With blinding speed, T'Challa zoomed past Sund and grabbed Zemo before he could jump. T'Challa rolled to the side, and the two men tumbled to the tarmac.

"Now that wasn't so bad, was it?" Ross said.

An hour later, something approaching order had been restored to the agency headquarters. Zemo had been returned to his cell and left with an armed guard.

Meanwhile, Charmagne Sund sat in a chair in Everett Ross's office. Ross himself stood outside the closed room, clutching Zemo's journal in his hands. T'Challa was with him, holding his Black Panther helmet tightly.

"I told you this would be easy," Ross said. He wasn't laughing—his voice was dripping with irony.

"So much pain," was all T'Challa could think to say. "The cycle of vengeance. It destroys everything."

Ross nodded.

"What will happen to her?" T'Challa asked, motioning with his head toward Ross's office, in which Charmagne Sund waited to hear her fate.

"We're in uncharted territory here," Ross said, shaking his head. "I've never had an agent try to take revenge on behalf of an entire country before."

"She was only doing what she thought was right," T'Challa countered. "She's a victim in all this, too."

"She is," Ross said, a trace of sympathy in his voice. "She's lucky she didn't hurt anyone. I'll see that she gets help. It's the least we can do for her."

Ross pointed with his hand toward the hallway. T'Challa started to walk, and Ross followed.

"We made a pretty good team, you and me," Ross said as they walked.

"A team?" T'Challa questioned. "Where were you while I was on the roof, trying to save two people?"

"Staying out of the way of you saving two people," Ross quipped.

T'Challa nodded. "So you are more helpful when you are not helping."

Ross thought about that for a moment. "Well, when you put it like that, it sounds like I did nothing."

EPILOGUE

For all his uncertainty, T'Challa was beginning to realize his father's wisdom. While he still believed that Wakanda must remain hidden, remain safe, he knew that the world at large needed protecting. It needed Black Panther. If nothing else, his time spent in the company of Everett Ross had proved that to him.

With men like Klaue and Zemo, whether Wakanda liked it or not, the world was out there, life was happening, and the lives of innocent people would always be at risk if brave people who had the means and technology to protect the world and rid it of evil did nothing.

He could not sit back and pretend that the violence was not happening.

Wakanda no longer had that luxury.

T'Challa no longer had that luxury.

From the cockpit of the Royal Talon Fighter, T'Challa

gazed out at the clouds above which he flew. He was finally headed home.

The call came in a moment later.

"Prince T'Challa," came a voice over his comm. "I need to ask for your help. It's about the Winter Soldier."

T'Challa recognized the voice immediately. It belonged to Steve Rogers.

Captain America.

"What can I do for you, Captain?" T'Challa asked.